We had two ropes around that horse, and he only had three feet free. None of it mattered. Demon raged and stormed. In an instant he tore one rope from my hands and nearly dragged Uncle Mitch from his horse. Pa hung on for dear life as Demon began bucking. That horse hopped in one direction, then another. I'd never seen such a show. Pa clung stubbornly to the animal's back close to five minutes. Then Demon threw him.

I raced over in order to shield Pa from the devil horse's dangerous hooves.

"I didn't do such a good job at it, eh, son?" Pa asked.

He was bruised and battered, but he assured me that no bones were broken.

"I suppose it's my turn now," I announced.

"No Alby!" Pa shouted.

"Alby, stop!" Uncle Mitch shouted.

They weren't either one of them in a position to halt me. I eased my horse alongside and jumped atop the devil horse. . . .

Mustang Flats

G. CLIFTON WISLER

Mustang Flats

PUFFIN BOOKS

PUFFIN BOOKS
Published by the Penguin Group
Penguin Putnam Books for Young Readers,
345 Hudson Street, New York, New York 10014, U.S.A.
Penguin Books Ltd, 27 Wrights Lane, London W8 5TZ, England
Penguin Books Australia Ltd, Ringwood, Victoria, Australia
Penguin Books Canada Ltd, 10 Alcorn Avenue, Toronto, Ontario, Canada M4V 3B2
Penguin Books (N.Z.) Ltd, 182-190 Wairau Road, Auckland 10, New Zealand

Penguin Books Ltd, Registered Offices: Harmondsworth, Middlesex, England

First published in the United States of America by Lodestar Books, an affiliate of
Dutton Children's Books, a division of Penguin Books USA Inc., 1997
Published by Puffin Books,
a member of Penguin Putnam Books for Young Readers, 1999

1 3 5 7 9 10 8 6 4 2

THE LIBRARY OF CONGRESS HAS CATALOGED THE LODESTAR EDITION AS FOLLOWS:
Wisler, G. Clifton
Mustang Flats / G. Clifton Wisler.—1st ed.
p.   cm.
Summary: When his father returns from the war in 1865, fourteen-year-old
Alby finds his beloved Pa a changed man and can only hope
that they will be friends again.
ISBN 0-525-67544-2 (hc.)
[1. Fathers and sons—Fiction. 2. Family life—Fiction. 3. United States—History—
Civil War, 1861–1865—Fiction.] I. Title
PZ7.W78033Mu 1997 96-29899 [Fic]—dc21 CIP AC

Puffin Books ISBN 0-14-130410-3

Printed in the United States of America

especially for Alan

It was dark, especially for April. I couldn't recall any night nearly as black. An odd chill filled the air, and clouds hid a full moon and most of the stars. That sort of evening was best passed indoors, with a roof to keep out the rain. Most times I liked life in the open, under the stars. You could feel all God's glory around you, and there were no little brothers to pester you halfway to death.

That night was different, though. It was just, well, me alone with me.

I frowned at the notion. Up on the hillside, I was about the highest thing for a good mile. In the daytime you could spot wagons or riders throwing up dust from the Preston road just west of us. Things being as they were, I could only make out the blurry shapes of two dozen sheep resting in the pasture below. Before the war we'd had fifty, and cattle as well. Six horses, too. That seemed a long time ago, though.

"At least it's not raining," I said as I struck the iron handle of my knife against a good piece of dark flint. Two sparks leaped onto a pile of dry leaves, and a small flame appeared. Soon a handful of dry twigs lit, too. I added some larger sticks. It wouldn't be much of a fire, but I dared not risk anything bigger, not with the grass midsummer dry. A bit of light would chase away some of the gloom. And fire kept critters at a distance.

Something stirred in the brush behind me. I rolled over to where I'd rested Pa's double-barreled shotgun. Before I could load it, a sharp *yip yip* announced my visitor. It was only Splinter.

"You cold, too?" I asked as the collie trotted over and began licking my fingers. "Sorry, boy. No treats today."

The dog barked a reply, and I moved back to the fire. I settled down beside the flickering flame, and Splinter lay across my feet. He was a lot of help, moving sheep around. He'd belonged to a neighbor, Colonel Stone, who had once owned hundreds of sheep. The colonel had high hopes for the three collie pups he'd bought off a Kentucky visitor. But the male pup just limped about, whimpering.

"Sore-footed," Colonel Stone frequently grumbled. "Useless."

I was only nine years old the first time I saw Splinter.

"Colonel, your dog's got a bad foot," I'd said. "Maybe I should have a look."

"That fool pup's got more than a sore foot, boy," the colonel told me. "Got two sisters with all the quality you expect in a collie, but that one is a waste of hide and bone."

Splinter hung his head, and I took a deep breath. It required gumption to speak up to somebody like

Colonel Stone, and I was pretty shy around people I didn't know well.

"I think he's a fine dog," I managed to say. "Bet I could mend his foot."

"Then you do it, Albert. Either way, the pup's yours."

Well, the colonel didn't expect Splinter to come to anything, and maybe I didn't, either. But I liked dogs, and a boy ought to have one. I led Splinter down to Spring Creek and had a good look at the sore paw. I didn't find anything right away. Later, though, I located a small sliver of wood buried in the poor pup's front left paw. Pa helped remove the splinter.

"Guess I've got myself a dog, Pa!" I'd cried afterward.

"You'd best take him back to Colonel Stone and explain," Pa replied. "A man doesn't take advantage of his neighbors."

I hung my head. It was just like Pa to send a dog back to Colonel Stone, who didn't even care enough for the pup to look him over proper! "Drapers don't ask for help, and they won't accept charity," he was fond of saying. "You do for yourself or go without."

So I trudged the half mile to the Stone place that next morning and explained about the splinter.

"Now he's not sore-footed, you'll probably want him back," I said, staring at my toes.

"You wouldn't be trying to go back on our bargain, would you?" Colonel Stone had asked.

"I don't think Pa'll allow it," I explained. "He's too fine a dog to take off you."

"Well, what do you think, pup?" Colonel Stone asked, turning to Splinter. The dog took to licking my

3

elbow, my arm, and finally my fingers. "Pup's made his choice, Albert. You tell your pa I insisted you have that dog."

Pa wasn't satisfied, though. He sent me back again, and I didn't convince him to let me keep the pup until I'd repaired two chicken coops and split half a wagon full of stovewood for Colonel Stone.

"Your pa can be a hard man to reason with," the colonel remarked.

"Yes, sir," I said. "He's got his ways, but they're not altogether bad ways."

"No, they're not," Colonel Stone agreed. "But there are times when neighbors ought to be able to do for each other."

I didn't argue. The way I figured things, it was best to stay out of range when grown people started philosophizing. In truth, I would have split three wagons full of wood and built a dozen coops to pay for that pup.

"You would've been a bargain even then," I said, scratching Splinter behind his ears. The collie was a better shepherd than Pa, me, and my three brothers put together!

As if to prove the point, Splinter suddenly tensed. Something rustled in the hackberry trees on the far side of the hill.

"Easy, boy," I said, stroking Splinter's shoulder with one hand while I reached for the shotgun with the other. Coyotes had taken a lamb the night before, and we couldn't spare another.

The noise was louder than a coyote, though. Heavier feet kicked up leaves, and a loud voice called, "Alby? You up here?"

I couldn't help laughing, and Splinter relaxed. It

4

was only John Tyler, my oldest brother. The skinny twelve-year-old spotted the fire and hurried over.

"Ma sent some stew," J. T. announced as he handed over a tin pot and a wooden spoon. "It's not half bad," he added as he set a leather bag beside the shotgun.

"Thanks," I said as I accepted the tin. It was only a third full. As I ate, I couldn't help remembering the feasts we'd enjoyed a few years earlier. Lately we never seemed to have enough so I could really feel satisfied.

"That's not possible anyway," Ma told me. "Not with growing boys."

Times had been hard for everyone. The war was going against the South. Rumors were flying around that the Yanks finally had General Lee on the run, that Richmond was lost, and that federal armies were landing all along the Texas coast.

"It's been for nothing," Ma had said between sobs the day after Ed Miller had returned from the East. His left leg was gone below the knee.

"What news of Hood's army?" Ma had asked.

"What army?" Miller had replied. "Most of it fell at Franklin, and the rest died at Nashville."

Ed Miller shared fearful tales of those battles.

"Do you know what happened to Frank?" Ma asked.

"He was with the Ninth, wasn't he?" Miller had said, scratching his head. "Most of 'em missed the charge at Franklin, but they suffered at Nashville. I saw Frank afterward, on a hill with some of the wounded."

"Was he hurt?" I asked.

5

"Hit in the leg, as I recall," Miller told us. "It's where they got me. Maybe he'll be back, too, before long."

Ed Miller had arrived in February. Now it was April.

"You're awful quiet, Alby," J. T. said, stoking the fire.

"Just thinking about Pa," I explained.

"You figure he'll come back?"

"Who knows?" I said, shrugging my shoulders.

"You get up to Sherman, though."

That was true enough. For a year and a half I had been carrying the mail up the road to Sherman and back. It gave me a chance to ride Grandpa French's gray gelding, and I picked up a few badly needed dollars, too.

"What do you think, Alby?" J. T. asked.

"Well, little brother, they get a newspaper or two in Sherman, but nobody seems to know what's happening. Grandpa says the South's finished, but you know he was born in Indiana. He wants the war over."

"Sometimes I can't remember what it was like before the fighting started," J. T. said. "Alby, I scarcely recall Pa. I'm not sure Jamie and Ben remember him at all."

"Four years is a long time, J. T. They were just babies."

"You were almost ten. Do you remember what it was like, Alby?"

"Easier," I said, cracking a smile as I licked the last of the stew from my spoon. "Easier than it's apt to ever be again."

J. T. rose to his feet and looked around a moment. Then he collected some brush and built up the fire.

"That's enough," I said when he started to add several larger sticks. "The grass's too dry."

"We need a little more light," he said, pulling a tattered mathematics primer from the leather bag.

"You could do your lessons back at the house, you know."

"*You* couldn't," he argued as he handed me the primer. "You promised Ma to keep up."

I nodded, and he added the sticks. Between tending to farm chores and carrying the mail, I had no time for school. I didn't have the patience for sitting still all day in a sweltering schoolroom anyway. I missed the company some, and I confess I enjoyed the adventures in some of the readers. But they didn't hold a candle to riding Grandpa's gelding.

J. T. drew two school slates out of the bag, and we worked through our ciphers. I finished mine quickly. I then oversaw J. T.'s work.

"I don't see how you can stay ahead when you don't even go to school anymore," J. T. grumbled when I corrected two mistakes.

"I've done most of this before," I explained. "Besides, numbers come easy to me."

I wished everything did.

J. T. was about finished with his ciphers when Splinter growled at the trees on the near side of the hill. I scrambled over to the shotgun and loaded a shell in each chamber.

"Coyotes?" J. T. asked as I gazed into the darkness.

"Most likely," I said, pulling Splinter closer. "I heard one howling earlier."

"What do we do?"

"*You* head back to the house and keep an eye on things there."

"Ah, Alby, you know Ma can shoot better'n I can. She won't ever let me do anything."

"I've only got one gun, J. T. It's dark as pitch here. I don't want anybody getting shot by mistake. Now get along home."

J. T. started to argue, but the sheep began bleating, and I had no more time.

"Go!" I shouted. Then, cradling the shotgun in my hands, I headed toward the trees.

Texas coyotes are sneaky smart. They won't come at a fellow head-on. No, they prefer skulking around in the shadows, looking for their chance to race in and kill a sheep. Our little herd was small enough as it was.

"Why us?" I called to the darkness. "Haven't we had enough trouble?"

Coyotes weren't known for soft hearts. One darted down the hill toward our sheep, and Splinter tore after it.

"Go, boy," I hollered.

Now, you wouldn't think a collie to be a true match for a coyote, but Splinter overtook that first critter and chased him clear of the herd. A second prowler approached from the other side of the sheep. When I started down that way, he retreated.

"Splinter, come on back," I called.

Splinter reluctantly abandoned his pursuit of the first coyote and dashed back to my side. He then turned toward a noise and growled.

"Easy," I said, readying the shotgun. "We can't chase shadows. Not with twenty sheep to watch."

We couldn't fire at shadows, either.

"Shot and powder's hard to come by," Ma had

8

scolded me the week before. Now she gave me only two shells, and I'd developed patience.

Splinter stood at my side, panting. We circled the sheep three times. I hoped the coyotes would grow discouraged, but when I rekindled the little fire, I heard them howling in the distance. It was going to be a long night.

It wasn't the first time I'd kept vigil on that hill. I'd lost track of the times I'd been there those past four years. In the beginning, Ma stayed with me. Later J. T. and I would take turns sleeping and watching. Now that I had some size, I managed it myself. After all, plenty of boys my age served in the army. I might have gone if Ma had anybody else to help with the farm. I couldn't help thinking of those other boys when I sat on the hill, minding the sheep. Compared to watching out for Yankees, guarding sheep seemed downright tame.

On toward midnight, the clouds broke up, and a few stars appeared overhead. I wondered if Pa could see those same stars way off in Tennessee or wherever he was. Ma thought he could. But now, after what Ed Miller had told us, I wasn't sure. Might be Pa wasn't coming home at all.

I'd missed him before, but never more than at that moment. I couldn't help remembering the time we'd found a dead calf down at Spring Creek. Coyotes had half eaten it. Even then the loss of an animal had been hard. Pa just nodded at the carcass and waved me along.

"Pa," I said, "shouldn't we hunt the coyotes?"

"For what?" he asked. "Being coyotes? Come over and sit with me a minute, Alby."

9

Pa wasn't what you'd call a well-read man, but he remembered everything he ever heard. He was fond of stories, and he especially favored fables. That morning at the creek he told me one about a scorpion. It was at a river and needed to get to the other side. When a frog happened by, the scorpion begged for a ride. The frog refused, fearing the scorpion might sting, but old Mr. Scorpion promised not to sting him. They started across the river just fine. Then, at the halfway point, that scorpion stung the frog. As the frog started to die, and the scorpion started to drown, the frog asked, "Why?"

"What'd he say, Pa?" I remembered asking. "Didn't the scorpion know he was going to die, too?"

"Sure, but you see, son, he was a scorpion. It was his nature to sting. The foolish one was the frog, who expected otherwise."

Pa managed a grin, but I was confused.

"What does that have to do with our dead calf, Pa?" I asked.

"Everything, Alby," he told me. "You can't expect a coyote not to be a coyote. And when they kill a calf or a lamb, you can't hate them for it. It's their nature, after all."

"Aren't you mad at them, Pa?"

"Ah, son, you might as well be mad at the moon for shining."

"I miss you, Pa," I told the stars overhead. "We need you. I'm no good at explaining coyotes or anything else. Ben and Jamie hardly remember you."

Splinter barked loudly, and I turned my attention to a shadow stepping out of the trees.

"Not tonight, coyote," I said, cocking the right-hand

10

hammer and aiming my shotgun. "I can't spare you a lamb. Go out and prowl somewhere else."

The coyote growled, and Splinter barked. I waved the dog to my side and took aim. "Maybe it's your nature to kill sheep," I called, "but I'm here to protect them."

I felt myself grow cold. My hands trembled a moment. Then they grew calm. The coyote moved closer, and I fired. Lead pellets blistered the hillside, and the creature yelped in pain. It dragged itself, dying, into the trees. Its companions howled, and the sheep bleated anxiously.

"I've got my nature, too, don't I?" I asked the stars. "Well, don't I?"

That next week things took a turn for the worse. We'd heard rumors of disasters before. Most of the time they were exaggerated. Not this time, though. I was making my Tuesday ride to Sherman, carrying the mail pouch from Grandpa French's store. Grandpa had served as postmaster before the war, and even though Colonel Stone's cousin Felix won the Confederate appointment, people still left their letters at the store. I took them to the stage depot, where Tom Thurman, the Sherman postmaster, passed them on. He gave me the southbound mail in return.

That particular day I found the depot crowded. Mr. Thurman was standing beside two Confederate colonels. The three of them were staring at some papers.

"A New Orleans newspaper," Bobby, the postmaster's fifteen-year-old son, explained. "We got two in this morning."

"I haven't seen a newspaper from New Orleans since '62," I said, wiping the sweat from my forehead on my shirtsleeve. "You sure?"

"I was the one who took the mail pouch," Bobby replied. "It carries hard news."

"What's happened?"

"General Lee's surrendered. Richmond's burned to the ground. Sherman's captured Joe Johnston's army in the Carolinas. We've lost, Alby."

"All that's happened?" I asked. "What about the western armies? What about—"

Bobby didn't have a chance to answer. His father and the colonels stepped out onto the depot's porch and announced to everyone the dreaded news. Lee had, indeed, surrendered. Others had followed suit.

"We received confirmation over the telegraph from Galveston," one of the colonels declared. "We're to await orders, but I'd say it's all over. You boys," he said, turning to a handful of soldiers loading a supply wagon, "can do what you think best. I'm going home."

The soldiers appeared stunned. They were all of them youngish, surely no more than nineteen. One of them unbuttoned his tunic and tossed it in the wagon. The others nodded and quit their work.

"Lord, what's next?" a gray-haired woman asked. "Will the Yankees come?"

"More'n likely," Mr. Thurman said, frowning. "But at least our boys'll get back home."

"Those still alive," Bobby added. His oldest brother, Delbert, had died at Murfreesboro, up in Tennessee. Two others were still alive when Ed Miller had left Nashville.

"I'll put this newspaper up in the window," Mr. Thurman told the crowd. "You can each of you see

13

what it says. It's a week old already. Who can say what's happened since?"

The others moved toward the window and waited for their chance to read the news. I paused while Mr. Thurman displayed the newspaper. Then I brought him the mail pouch.

"Thanks, Alby," he said, thumbing through the letters. "We won't be running any more mail now. Not until the Yankees come."

"Sir?" I asked.

"The government won't survive, Alby. Confederate appointments will mean nothing."

"Mr. Thurman, I need the money really bad," I pleaded. "People will still want their letters sent."

"Alby, I could only pay you with Confederate money. It's worthless."

"Worthless?" I gasped. I had close to fifty dollars saved up. Pa owned several thousand dollars' worth of government bonds, too.

"Here," Mr. Thurman said, handing me his cashbox. I counted six hundred and seventy-two dollars. "Take it," he urged. "Maybe you can use it to write out your lessons."

I stared at the notes. I couldn't move. How could money lose its value overnight? I pocketed the bills and turned to go.

"Here, don't leave empty-handed, Alby," Mr. Thurman pleaded. "A man ought to be paid for his work." He pulled out a box and rummaged through it. He found a small tin of brass buttons, five yards of gray cloth, and a good hunting knife. "Confederate property," he explained. "You might help yourself to a keg of molasses off that wagon outside, too. By nightfall there won't be anything left in the warehouse. Too many hereabouts are in need."

"Yes, sir," I agreed. "Seems a little like stealing, though, doesn't it?"

"They were our goods before the government took them. Better we make use of what's left than leave it for the Yankees."

I nodded. I did take a keg of molasses, and one of the soldiers offered me a coarse cotton blanket. I tied the keg to my saddle horn and secured the blanket and cloth behind me. Then I watered the gelding and started home.

I spread the dark news of Lee's surrender as I went. Nobody seemed very surprised. Grandpa French nodded soberly. Then he furled the flag he flew outside the store and stowed it in his back room.

"Is it true our money's no good now?" I asked, pulling the Confederate notes from my pocket.

"They haven't been worth much for almost a year," Grandpa said. "I've been taking them, of course, but only at three cents' value on the dollar."

"Could I get three cents a dollar for these?" I asked, showing him the bills.

"Alby, they aren't worth three cents altogether."

"And Pa's bonds?"

"I warned Frank against buying them. You'll not see a dime's worth of value for them. Do you have any greenbacks left from before the war? Coins?"

"I don't know," I said, hanging my head. "Not likely. We've been selling stock to get by."

"Well, paper money's never much comfort, son. You've got stock, and the government won't be coming through here taking your crops like last year."

"No, sir," I replied. "We've got our corn growing. Folks can get by on cornmeal and mutton if they have to."

I stayed another hour at Grandpa's. Partly it was because I wanted to give the gray a good brushing, that being our last ride to Sherman and all. I also earned two silver dimes helping Grandpa restock his shelves. He agreed to bring the molasses and blanket the next time he drove his wagon to the farm. I took the cloth and buttons with me.

It was three miles up Spring Creek to our place. All along the way I practiced what I would say to Ma. It wouldn't be easy. We'd faced hard news before, of course. The war brought little else. But since Ed Miller's return, we'd all hoped and prayed that Pa would come home alive. Now, if the war was over, it seemed less likely. Even if he did, how would we get by? Those bonds were all the security Ma had. We'd sold our cattle. The Confederate quartermasters had taken last year's wheat and left us paper vouchers. We couldn't swap them for sawdust!

I hadn't wanted to scream as much in I don't know how long. I was tempted to cry, but a boy closing in on his fourteenth birthday doesn't do that. I swallowed my bitterness and walked faster. I got to the house a half hour before dinner.

"You're back on time for once," Ma remarked. "What's wrong? Couldn't you find any distractions in Sherman?"

"Not many," I told her as I set the cloth on the porch and drew the tin of buttons from my pocket.

"What do you have here?" she asked. "Uniform cloth? Alby, we've talked about this. I won't sew you a uniform so you can join the army."

"Isn't any army left," I said, sighing. "Ma, it's all over. Lee's surrendered, and Richmond's lost."

"Lee's not the only general fighting for the Southern cause," she said. "Your father's—"

"Ma, they're hauling in flags and sending the soldiers home. Look," I said, taking the Confederate notes from my pocket. "They're giving away money. It's not worth anything."

Ma turned pale.

"Our bonds, Alby. They have to honor those bonds."

"Ma, if paper money's no good, those bonds—"

"Lord help us," she said, pulling me to her side.

That night at supper we said a special prayer for Pa and the other soldiers. Then Ma passed a bowl of cornmeal muffins around.

"We're going to have a difficult time," she told us. "We're Drapers, though. We've known trials before, and we've passed through each and every storm. We'll weather this one."

I studied my brothers. Ben was only eight, and he couldn't remember an easy time. I don't suppose he understood what had changed. Jamie was ten now. He knew he didn't have shoes to wear to school like most of his classmates. J. T., well, he may have looked scrawny for a twelve-year-old, but he held up his end.

"The important thing to remember," Ma said softly, "is that the land provides for us. We have pasture for our sheep and good soil for our crops."

"We'll do fine," J. T. boasted. "Corn's growing taller and faster than ever. Alby and I'll thin out the plants this week."

"It should have been done already," she observed. "But this week will do."

"Sorry," I said, lowering my gaze. "There's been a lot of work, what with the coyotes and all."

"That's one problem we'll solve immediately," she said.

"Ma?"

"The sheep will have to go, Alby. We can't manage them and the corn, and livestock will still fetch a price. I'll speak to Mrs. Stone. Perhaps she can make us a reasonable offer."

"Nobody's got any money, not Yankee money," J. T. said. "Of course, Alby and I could take the sheep to Dallas, see if anybody there would buy them."

"You'll be needed in the fields," Ma insisted. "I'll attend to the sale. Surely we can get a few cows. Milk and cheese would be of more use to us than wool just now. Less bother, too. Perhaps we could have a few cowhides. We'll all of us need shoes come winter."

"Yes, ma'am," I agreed.

The rest of April and all of May passed before any of us felt very hopeful. Miranda Stone had little of the colonel's generosity, and Ma swapped fifteen of our sheep to Edgar Hutchison up on Rowlett Creek for four milk cows, five good cowhides, and two butter churns. Some money was promised as well. We clipped the other five sheep before turning them over to Grandpa. He planned to butcher them and sell the meat to town folk.

That spring a strange sort of cloud hung over northern Texas. Confederate flags vanished. Judges, sheriffs, postmasters, and clerks closed their offices and went to work tending crops and livestock. The school closed down so boys and girls could help in the fields. Children who had passed free afternoons fishing at the creek often as not now provided their families with a perch or catfish for dinner.

By May the first returning soldiers began to trickle into Collin County. My heart leaped every single time I spied a gray coat or a dusty slouch hat. But when I got closer, I failed to see any familiar faces.

"Don't you know me, Alby?" a dark-eyed, thin-faced fellow cried one afternoon. Splinter growled, and I felt my legs wobble. "Look at me, son," he said. "I'm your Uncle Mitch!"

I shrank back in horror. Mitchell French had helped me train Splinter to herd sheep. Back then he'd been a smiling, shaggy-haired fellow, full of pranks and patient as a circling buzzard.

"Alby?" he called.

I took a deep breath and gripped his hands. He felt weak as a kitten.

"I'll help you to Grandpa's," I offered.

"Be shorter to your place," he said. "Maybe you could loan me a horse."

"Don't have one," I answered. "The quartermaster took the two Pa left us."

"We can get a mount at my place," a second man suggested. I had to stare hard before realizing it was Colonel Stone.

"You've had some hard times," I observed.

"We've got all our parts, Alby," Uncle Mitch replied. "We're home."

"Things haven't been that easy for you here, either," the colonel said. "See you've raised that pup into a fine dog."

"Splinter does his share of work. Of course, now that we've got no more sheep, he mostly hunts rabbits."

19

"I haven't seen any cows, either," Uncle Mitch noted. "Quartermasters take them, too?"

"No, but they took most of the county's wheat," I told them. "We're trying to get by until Pa returns."

Colonel Stone sighed, and Uncle Mitch wrapped an arm around my shoulder the way he had when I was little.

"Alby, your Pa was shot pretty bad," Uncle Mitch said, trembling. "We left him in Tennessee when we marched south to Mobile. I don't know if he's alive. Chances are if he was, he'd been back before now."

"Sure," I said, swallowing hard. "I know. Just don't go saying that to Ma. She's still praying he'll be back. You don't know he won't."

"No, we don't," Colonel Stone said. "It's the best thing, Albert, holding out hope. But if you reach the point, you and your mother, where you've come to the end of your tether, pay me a call. Promise me that?"

"Yes, sir," I answered, even though I knew Ma would never invite a neighbor's help. She was as hard as Pa on that account.

Uncle Mitch's return brightened Ma some. I don't think she was any more hopeful that Pa would come back, but having her brother home cheered her. Grandpa thought Mitch's homecoming merited a celebration. He and my cousin Maureen rode out in a wagon to invite us to a family gathering at Uncle Mitch's farm.

"I don't know," I said, avoiding her eyes. "We've got a lot of work to do."

"Nonsense," Grandpa declared. "It's about time Amanda and you boys had some fun."

"We hardly ever see you," Maureen complained. She was just three months younger than I was, and once upon a time we'd been like two peas from the same pod.

"Well, you know I had to give up going to school," I told her.

"Nobody's going to school these days," she reminded me. "Our place isn't an hour's walk down Spring Creek. We used to swim in July."

"Well, some things've changed since those days," I said, grinning.

She looked down at her chest and blushed.

"Pa will want you to come," she said as Grandpa stepped down from the wagon. He had the keg of molasses and the blanket in back. I took the keg and allowed him to tote the blanket.

Ma stepped out to greet them then, and she agreed that a family gathering was a fine idea.

"I'll bake a pie," she announced.

I gave her a warning glance, but Maureen was ahead of me.

"Oh, don't bother bringing food, Aunt Amanda," Maureen said, laughing. "Colonel Stone's promised to butcher a calf, and Ma's been baking for three days. Much as we'd value one of your pies, I wish you'd wait a couple of weeks. The Methodist circuit rider's due to start his rounds again next Sunday. Maybe we could join you up here after worship."

"Would seem best, dear," Grandpa told Ma.

"Maybe," she said. I believed she realized that the sugar bowl was empty. And cornmeal was a poor substitute for wheat flour where pie crust was concerned.

"You could bring some flowers," Maureen suggested. "Alby used to find some pretty ones."

"He did?" Ma asked. "I never knew he was much of a flower picker."

"Took them to Eula Mae Hutchison," Maureen said, fighting the urge to smile. "I think he was in love with her or something."

"Alby?" Grandpa asked.

"Eula Mae's grown a head taller than me now," I said. "Besides, who's got the time for girls?"

"I didn't know a boy could be *that* busy," Ma said, winking at me.

"This one can," I growled. "I remember where the flowers are, though. Rose of Sharon and some others."

"We'll enjoy them," Maureen assured me.

I left to stow the molasses then, but Ma passed close to an hour talking with Grandpa. Afterward she announced that J. T. would start to work at the store.

"I could've done it," I complained.

"We can spare John Tyler easier than you, Alby," Ma explained. "Once he's better at his figures, Jamie can go."

"I can?" Jamie asked.

"You're old enough," she said. "Your grandfather's not as young as he used to be. Now that Mama's dead, he has a hard time running the store alone. Eben's been helping."

My cousin Eben was just ten, Jamie's age. Now that Uncle Mitch was home, Grandpa probably figured Eben wouldn't need to earn extra money.

"So that's settled," she said, nodding. She went on to tell about the family gathering at Uncle Mitch's place. "Alby's provided a keg of molasses, so I think I'll bake some cookies. We can manage that at least."

I knew it rankled Ma that we were so short of everything. Mr. Hutchison owed us money for the sheep, but he had not yet had a chance to travel anywhere he could sell animals for Yankee greenbacks. Even then, she'd never spend that money for anything we could do without. No, we'd have to harvest our corn before we could consider buying coffee or sugar, much less shoes and such. The gray cloth made simple shirts and trousers for my brothers, but I had a decent pair of overalls already. My shirt was growing ragged, but I was hopeful my birthday would provide a replacement.

Uncle Mitch's homecoming gave us all a welcome break from chores and worries. It turned out half the families along Spring Creek came. Colonel Stone saw to the roasting of his beeve, and everyone brought something to complete the dinner. I hadn't seen such plenty in four summers! My brothers and I ate mounds of potatoes, carrots, and roast beef. We gorged ourselves with cookies and fresh peaches. It was a feast!

After eating, I headed down to the creek with the other boys. J. T., Jamie, Eben, and Ben shed their clothes and splashed into the shallows. I sat on a hillside and chatted with Matt Price, my best friend since the two of us met ten summers before while skipping rocks in the creek.

"I'm glad your uncle came back," Matt said as he offered me a peach slice.

"Sure," I said, gazing westward. "I wish Pa'd get here."

"That would make it easier," he said as he cut a slice for himself. "You know mine was killed at Chickamauga."

"Yes," I told him. "It's a hard thing to say, but I don't know that you aren't the lucky one. At least you know for sure. Sometimes I wish—"

"No, you don't," Matt barked. "Don't ever wish that. Jake Miller's pa may only have one leg, but he's there to show him how to use a razor. There's so much—"

"You don't need a razor yet," I told him. "When you do, I'll show you how to use one."

"You?" he gasped. "There's more fuzz on this peach than on your chin."

24

"Maybe, but I'm getting taller."

"So am I," Matt declared, standing up and stretching himself. I suppose I had three or four inches on him, but I stooped a bit to make it appear less.

"You ever wonder what'll become of us, Matt?" I asked, studying the countryside. It seemed so empty. The closest thing to a road running east and west was little better than a trail scratched by wagon rims. Even the Preston road turned to goo during a decent rain. I recalled Pa's tales of Nashville, New Orleans, and the old walled cities he'd seen during the war in Mexico.

"I've got to stay home for a time yet," Matt told me. "Ma will insist on it. Later, I figure maybe I'll chase horses or cattle out west. Pa went up to Kansas in '57 and filled his pockets with greenbacks."

"You can't make money selling cows that you don't have," I pointed out. "Or ride a horse you don't own."

"No, guess not," Matt said. "Still, I hear there's plenty of horses running loose over in Denton County. We could rope a few."

"Barefoot?"

"Well, we'd have to be good at it."

"Have to be crazy," I said, laughing. "Any horse worth owning would drag you to Dallas and back. A man needs to be mounted to rope mustangs."

"Then I guess we'd best figure out a way to get some mounts."

I started to tell him just how crazy a notion that was, but Splinter raced up, yelping furiously. I glanced to the west and froze. The wind was up, and I had an odd sensation down my spine.

"Thunderheads," Matt whispered, pointing to the sky.

"J. T.!" I yelled. "We best start home!"

He was already splashing his way to the bank. Ben, Jamie, and Eben followed. They were throwing their clothes on while Matt and I raced back to the house to alert the others.

There was no need. Women hurried about, collecting dishes and dragging chairs indoors. The men were readying wagons or climbing atop their horses.

"You'd best wait here, Alby," Uncle Mitch shouted. "That's a bad storm. Maybe a cyclone even."

"I have to see to the animals," I said.

"Alby, wait," Ma called. I gazed hard into her eyes, and she waved me on along. She understood the need. Grandpa offered me his gray, but the horse was skittish in a storm.

"Splinter, stay with Ma," I said, pointing to her. Then I ran as fast as I could toward home.

Matt accompanied me as far as his place. I went the rest of the way alone. By then, the rain was coming down in sheets. J. T. arrived as the first hailstones battered the barn.

"Ma sent me," he explained as we huddled together on the porch. "She didn't figure you could get the cows to cover on your own."

"I didn't," I said, watching helplessly as they bawled. I took a deep breath and splashed across the farmyard to the barn. I dragged the heavy door open, and the cows hurried in. J. T. was behind them, whacking their rumps with a stick.

I paused a moment to catch my breath. That was when I heard the train.

Now I'll confess that I'd only heard stories of locomotives. I'd neither seen nor heard one. But the sound, well, I recognized it from stories.

"Sounds just like a freight train," Pa had told me a hundred times. "Cyclones. One comes, you find yourself the deepest cover at hand."

"Where to?" J. T. asked.

"Root cellar," I replied.

"Alby, we don't have a root cellar," J. T. objected.

"I know, little brother, and we don't have time to dig one."

Instead, we raced outside and made our way to a rocky cut in the side of the hill just past the house. We crouched there, waiting for the cyclone to do its worst. By then we could spot it clearly. A skinny finger of dark cloud danced about like a waterspout. It seemed to cut an uneven path along the creek bottom. It stayed a quarter of a mile away, but the winds it brought clawed at the shingles of the house and tore planks off the barn. Once it passed, the hail worsened. All I could do was cover my head and wince each time a big one smashed my elbows or knees. J. T. howled beside me, and together we hurled every curse and insult we knew at that storm.

I don't suppose the whole thing lasted more than an hour. The ground was coated with icy pellets, and pieces of trees and plants were strewn everywhere. I stumbled to my feet and helped J. T. up. Together we limped to the house.

It was a mess. Every window on the western side of the house was broken. One of the porch columns had snapped, and that part of the roof hung at a crazy angle.

The barn fared better, and the animals appeared all

right. One of the chickens lay dead, but the rest had survived.

"Wasn't so bad," J. T. said as he peeled off his shirt and wrung the water out of it. His back was peppered with round, red marks left by the hail.

"Not so bad?" I cried, staring at the roof.

"You remember that time lightning burned the west pasture? We lost half our wheat."

"The corn," I said, shuddering. "J. T., you ever see what hail does to plants?"

He shook his head, but I hardly noticed. I was already on my way to the fields. By the time he caught up, I was walking down the rows, screaming at the unfairness of it all. There weren't enough stalks left standing to bother with.

"Alby?" J. T. called. "Alby, what'll we do?"

"I don't know," I said, dropping to my knees. I just sat there, clawing at the ground. I was in a trance, I suppose. Splinter finally raced over and began licking my face. It brought me back to my senses.

"He's gone crazy," I heard J. T. tell Ma. "Look at him."

I managed to stand up before Ma arrived.

"We've lost the crop, haven't we?" she asked.

"Yes, ma'am," I answered. "Ma, I don't know what to do."

"We'll manage," she assured me. "We always have."

I didn't see how, though. J. T. and I went from farm to farm those next few days. We hired ourselves out to anyone willing to pay. One day we boarded up broken windows. The next we burned dead animal carcasses. We made two dollars altogether.

28

I turned fourteen the last day of July, but I didn't expect any celebration. We were all too busy to stop. Ma fooled me, though. When I returned from mending one of Colonel Stone's coops, I found Uncle Mitch, Aunt Lottie, Maureen, and Eben waiting. Grandpa was inside, and Matt appeared shortly afterward with a parcel under one arm.

"Happy birthday," he said, passing the present into my hands.

I peeled off the paper and found two hand-sewn moccasins.

"At least you won't be barefoot," he told me.

J. T. presented a miniature Splinter carved out of oak, and Ma gave me one of Pa's old shirts cut down to fit. Maureen brought a fresh-baked peach pie, and Uncle Mitch handed me a deerskin hip scabbard for my Confederate knife.

"Wish it could be more," Grandpa whispered as he placed two silver dollars in my hand. "Things'll be better next year."

Better? Maybe different, but better?

That night before he left, Grandpa spoke with Ma about selling the farm.

"You can come and run the store for me, Amanda," he said. "It supported a family once. It can again."

"Frank will expect us to have the farm waiting when he gets home," she argued. "The boys need room to run and grow. They're better off here."

"They're working themselves half to death," Grandpa complained. "They're past thin. You know that. Winter will bring sickness. Hunger. Is that what you want? And what about taxes? How will you pay them?"

"We'll manage, God willing."

"And if He's not willing?"

"Then we'll no doubt have this discussion again, Papa. We'll wait a bit longer for Frank."

"I hope you still have choices later," he told her.

"There are always choices, Papa," she insisted.

I doubted even then that there were many good ones.

I was standing on what was left of the porch, staring at the darkening horizon, when she joined me.

"Sometimes I think you must be eighty years old," she said, laughing. "You look awfully serious. What worries you so?"

"What doesn't?" I asked.

"I see you like this, and it puts me in mind of your father."

"Ma, I hardly remember what he looks like."

"I never have that trouble, Alby. I just look at you, and Frank's there. You're his image, you know."

"I am?"

I'd always known I didn't take after Ma. She and my brothers had dark brown hair and green eyes. My hair had always been yellowish blond, although lately it was taking on a kind of chestnut brown tint. My eyes were blue, like Pa's. I did recall that much.

"I know it's been hard, Alby. Especially on you," she told me.

"No harder on me than you."

"I'm your mother. It's a woman's lot to worry over her family."

"When Pa left, he told me I was the man of the house. I was supposed to tend things, but I've made a mess of it."

"You did what you could. No one can hold off hail."

"I should've done better, Ma."

"No one could have expected that," she said, pulling me to her side. "We're all of us alive, aren't we? Nobody's died."

"Nobody?" I asked.

"Nobody," she insisted. "He's coming home, Alby."

I didn't hold out much hope of it, but I said nothing.

The following afternoon I was down at the creek, cutting scrub cedars to make new shingles for the roof, when Splinter started barking. I set down my ax and located Uncle Mitch driving Grandpa's wagon along the creek. It was odd, him coming over two days in a row.

"Alby!" Uncle Mitch shouted. "J. T.! Come see who's here."

I waved J. T. toward the creek. Then I followed. At first I didn't see what Uncle Mitch was talking about. Then a tired-eyed stick of a boy rose from the wagon bed. Most of his left ear was gone, his pants were no better than patched rags, and his shirt was little more than a yellow-brown collar with tatters attached.

"Meet Nebo Hill," Uncle Mitch said.

I offered my hand, but Nebo was using his to help a gaunt, one-legged horror out of the wagon.

"Who is it?" J. T. whispered.

I just stood there, not quite believing it. His face was old as sin and gray as death, but I recognized the blue blaze in his eyes.

"Pa?" I gasped.

"Alby, is that you?" he said between wheezes. "Nebo, this is my boy."

31

Nebo then took my hand and gave it a hard squeeze.

"He's been worse," the boy explained. "Near died on me twice, but I swore I'd see him home."

"Home?" Pa muttered. He managed to stiffen his back, and with Nebo's help, he crawled out of the wagon. "Same old creek," he said, dipping a bare toe in the stream. "John Tyler?"

"Yes, sir?" J. T. asked.

"You've grown some, too. Be needing a razor soon."

"See, Alby?" J. T. said, elbowing my ribs. "Told you."

"Let's get along to the house now, Nebo," Pa urged. "Wouldn't want to keep Amanda waiting."

"No, Frank," Nebo agreed.

"We can take the wagon," I suggested. "Uncle Mitch—"

"Has done enough," Pa barked. "Thank you anyway, Mitchell, but I need to give the leg some work."

"I'll be around, Alby, if you need anything," Uncle Mitch promised.

"Now I'm home, we won't be needing anything," Pa declared. "Give Lottie and the children my best."

"I will," Uncle Mitch said.

"It's a fair way to the house, Pa," I reminded him.

"I haven't been away so long that I'd forget my own farm," Pa grumbled. "Walked here from Tennessee, didn't I? I expect I can manage."

J. T. and I moved aside as Nebo slid a wooden crutch under Pa's arm. They then started toward the house.

"He scares me," J. T. said after they'd gone.

"I know," I admitted. "It's just the war, though. He's had a long, hard march from Tennessee. Once he's washed and gets some of Ma's cooking, he'll cheer up."

"Hope so, Alby. 'Cause right now he could frighten the bark off a tree!"

It was strange, having Pa back. It wasn't at all like I expected it would be. He barely said three words to J. T. or me, and he pretty much ignored Jamie and Ben.

"Did we do something wrong?" Jamie asked.

"Of course not," Ma said, pulling him to her side. "Your pa's tired. He's had a difficult time just getting here. He's used to the army. We have to let him get reacquainted with us."

I don't think any of us understood that. Reacquainted? He was our father, wasn't he?

Ma was right, though. Pa was a stranger. We didn't know him at all. That next morning Ma was up early, cooking breakfast. I was only halfway awake myself, and J. T. had to shake me to life.

"Pa's an early riser," he said, pointing to the yellow-orange eastern horizon.

I was, too, generally, but I usually waited for the roosters to crow. While J. T. roused Ben and Jamie, I slipped into my overalls and hurried out to fill the water barrel. When I stepped into the kitchen with the first bucket of well water, Ma poured half of it into a kettle. I went back to the well, refilled the bucket, and returned.

"Your pa's out in the barn," Ma explained as she poured hot water into a small basin. "He's having a wash. Take him the hot water, Alby."

"Yes, ma'am," I said. I deemed it good news. Even though he and Nebo had traded their rags for some of Pa's old clothes, Pa still needed cleaning up and a shave. I hurried to the barn, but I hardly got inside the door.

"Ah, the water," Pa growled. "Give it to Nebo."

"I can bring it over," I offered.

"Give it to Nebo," Pa insisted. "Go on and have your breakfast. You have chores waiting."

I handed Nebo the basin and retreated to the kitchen. By then J. T., Jamie, and Ben were sitting at the table. Ma brought in a platter of eggs and corn bread.

"James, it's your turn to say grace," she said, nodding to Jamie.

"Lord, for all Your bounty, we thank You," Jamie prayed.

"And?" Ma asked.

Jamie appeared confused, and Ma scowled.

"Thank you for sending Frank home to us," Ma added.

We boys hadn't been too sure about the bounty part, and we were even less certain about our father. It got no better when he and Nebo joined us.

"No bacon?" Pa said, studying the table. "When did we start having breakfast without side meat?"

"Things have been hard lately," Ma answered.

"I didn't see the stock. I guess they're in the back pasture."

"Frank, the government took our crop last year. We had to sell off the cattle. I sold the sheep, too."

"Why?"

"Because after the surrender, no one honored Confederate money. We needed things."

"Still do," Pa said, gazing around at the broken windows. "Well, summer's half gone. Corn'll be ready for harvest before too long."

I stared at my empty plate. It was quieter than midnight just then.

"Well, what is it?" Pa asked.

"We can't count on the corn, Pa," I said nervously. "We had a storm, and, well, the plants were—"

"So, we've got no crop, no stock, nothing?" Pa backed away from the table and tried to rise. He fumbled with his crutch, though, and almost fell. Nebo leaped to his feet and helped Pa right himself.

"Frank?" Ma cried.

Pa ignored her. "Albert!" he shouted, pointing to the door.

"No, Alby," Jamie said, grabbing my arm.

I squeezed his hand and went on outside. I felt a little like a man stepping toward a firing squad, but I couldn't see how things could get a lot worse. I was wrong. Pa pushed me against the wall and stared hard into my eyes.

"Albert, I can't believe you've let things come to this," he told me. "Even in the worst drought, we always made a corn crop. Do you remember what I told you before I left?"

"Yes, sir," I said, shifting my weight from foot to foot.

"Well?"

"I was to look after things."

"You did a fine job of it, didn't you? Just look at this place. The roof's torn to pieces. The barn has planks missing. The stock's gone, and we've got no crop. And what about your brothers! Barefoot and in rags. They look worse than the Army of Tennessee on its worst day, and that's pretty bad, son. How could you let things come to this?"

"I tried, Pa," I said, hanging my head. "I took on any work I could find. I saved up some money carrying the mail to and from Sherman, but it was all Confederate. Nobody puts any value in it now. I'm sorry. I did my best."

"Wasn't very good, was it?" he asked.

"No, sir."

I half expected him to hit me or at least to lay down some punishment. Instead, he shook his head and hobbled off to the barn.

"It's only the pain talking, Alby," Ma told me later. "He couldn't know how difficult things would be for us. Nobody could expect a boy ten years old to shoulder a man's load. Once he realizes how hard you've worked, he'll take those harsh words back. There isn't another boy I know who could have done as well."

"Ma, will we have to sell the farm?"

"What?"

"I heard Grandpa talking. Taxes will come due, and we've no money."

"We'll have some from the sheep," she explained.

"Then what will we eat this winter?"

"That's no worry of yours," she said, brushing the hair back from my forehead. "I know it's going to be difficult, but try to be a boy again for a time."

"And Pa?"

"You're not the only one I talk to," she said, kissing my forehead. "Give your pa some time. Now see if you can't help your brothers with their chores."

I started toward the barn, but J. T. blocked my path.

"Pa says you should feed the chickens," he told me.

"That's your job," I argued.

"Not today," J. T. said, grinning slightly. "Pa said he wanted to find something he was sure you could do. It's not like before, Alby. You're not boss anymore."

I glared at him, and J. T. dashed off to safer ground. I located the chicken feed, filled a small bag, and set off toward the coop.

Bad as that morning was, it was only the beginning. Those next few days weren't any better. Pa stormed around the farm all day, complaining that this or that hadn't been done. When I told him I had been splitting cedar logs into shingles to repair the roof, he nearly bit my head off. "That should have been done months ago!" he shouted.

Nights were worst of all. If he wasn't wheezing, he was coughing. The wall between the room he and Ma shared and we boys' room was too thin to hide sounds. Twice he woke up screaming. Each time he'd walk out to the barn and pass the rest of the night there, with Nebo.

"It's just the war coming back to him," Ma told us. "It will pass."

I spent most of my time that August repairing the roof. Uncle Mitch came over to supervise the work, but once I proved up to the job, he left me to it. Later Pa helped replace the broken porch post. It was the first time we'd shared a task, and it proved to be a trial. I never did anything well enough to merit approval. Pa, one-legged as he was, couldn't do it himself, though, and J. T. wasn't big enough.

Once we finished, the house was in better condition. We couldn't replace the broken windows yet because glass was too expensive. It was too hot to board them over, and we settled for covering them with cheesecloth.

"Now it can rain again," J. T. declared after dinner one night. "Wish it would, too, just to settle the dust."

Ma had a different sort of announcement.

"I visited with Jenny Price this afternoon," she said. "She's going to open a school next week. I assured her you boys would be attending."

"How will we be paying for this?" Pa asked.

"With sewing," Ma answered. "I've attended to it myself, Frank."

"Well, I suppose it's best the boys continue their schooling," Pa said.

"I thought I was going to help Grandpa," J. T. objected.

"That's all changed now," Ma said.

"I thought I might hire out," I said, turning to Pa. "I'm good with horses, and Splinter and I can mind sheep."

"You'll go to school," Pa muttered. "Maybe you'll learn about work there."

I felt like a dagger had just ripped through my heart. I started to say something, but Ma flashed a warning glance, and I swallowed the words.

A few days later we boys were swimming off the afternoon wearies in the cooling waters of Spring

Creek. Uncle Mitch and Eben joined us. Matt came over later. We splashed and raced and laughed away the August heat.

Afterward Matt and I took turns tossing sticks to Splinter.

"You hear that Ma's opening a school?" he finally asked.

"My ma told us," I said, throwing a twig. "My brothers will go. Me, I'm not so sure. I've been thinking of finding work."

"Hiring out?"

"Yes. We're short of cash, and I could help some."

"Don't you think your pa needs you at the farm?"

"I figure he values me less than those Confederate bonds he bought," I said. "Lots of boys fourteen years old head off on their own. Maybe it's time I did, too."

"I thought you'd be glad to hear about the school."

"We need so many things, Matt."

"It's not your job to pay the taxes, Alby. Leave your pa and ma to worry over that."

"It's not just the money, Matt. I don't feel welcome anymore. Pa's lost faith in me."

"Then he doesn't know you."

"Does that make it any better?" I asked.

"Guess not," Matt admitted. "Still, it would be nice having you back at school."

I nodded to him. He tossed the stick to Splinter two more times. Then he waved farewell and headed back across the creek to his place. I walked a little farther upstream and began skipping flat stones across the stream.

"I used to do that," a voice called from behind me. It was Nebo.

"Didn't notice you," I said somewhat apologetically.

"I walk softly," he explained. "A soldier's habit," he added as he stepped to the creek. Nebo dipped his head in the stream and pulled it back out.

"Texas is hotter'n Mississippi," he exclaimed.

"My brothers and I cool off here," I told him. "They're downstream a couple of hundred yards."

"Saw 'em," Nebo said.

"Pa figures you're part of the family. I don't think anybody would mind you—"

"It's not that."

"No?"

"You see how folks stare at my ear. It's not intended, but they do it. They're not altogether comfortable around me."

"Oh," I said, growing uneasy. "They shot you up pretty bad, huh?"

"At Franklin, south of Nashville," Nebo said. "I was a bugler, although my regiment wasn't mounted anymore. The Yanks were entrenched on a rise, and we ran right at 'em. They could see us coming, and they shot us to pieces. I was hit twice. Then a shell knocked me senseless. I was drifting off on a cloud with my ma and pa and my little brother Henry.

"I don't know how long I lay there, bleeding and dying. Then two strong arms lifted me up and carried me like a baby off the field. I woke up later in the camp of the Ninth Texas Infantry. It was your pa who saved me, and he tended me day and night, bringing me back to life. The surgeons wanted to discharge me, but I'm from Vicksburg. My whole family died in the siege. I had nowhere better to go, and the Ninth was shorthanded. I stuck with them.

41

"We marched up to Nashville and threatened the Yanks there. They turned the tables on us and attacked. Frank lost his leg, and I stuck by him. We were captured, but we survived."

"I guess we all owe you a debt, Nebo," I told him.

"No, I'm the debtor. First Frank gave me back my life. Then he gave me a place to belong. Problem is, I think maybe it was your place. I never intended stealing it from you."

"Isn't your fault," I told him.

"Nor yours," he insisted. "Alby, give your pa some time to forget. We both saw things you can't imagine."

"That's not my fault, either. I wanted to join the army, but they said I was too young. Later, boys no older'n me signed up, but Ma wouldn't allow me to."

"Be glad," Nebo said, shuddering.

"I've seen a few things," I told him.

"Then maybe you're ready for this," he said, stripping off his shirt. A dreadful scar ran from under his left arm along his side to the hip. A reddish stain spread across his belly.

"Burn," Nebo said, rubbing his stomach. "From a shell fragment. There's more."

He loosened his trousers, and when they dropped, I saw scars on his right thigh and hip.

"Those are the ones easily seen," Nebo said. "There are others."

"Others?" I asked.

"Inside, where they stay hidden. Your pa's got those, too."

"Is that why he wakes up screaming?"

"Why a lot of soldiers do," he told me. "You'd hear me, too, if I wasn't in the barn."

"What does Pa see in his dreams?"

"That's something he'll have to tell you, Alby. I hope he will, too."

I wasn't very hopeful of it. In truth, I wasn't sure that I really wanted to know.

If it had been up to me, I wouldn't have gone to Mrs. Price's school. It wasn't. Ma turned a deaf ear to every single one of my protests. Pa deemed it best I shepherd my brothers there and insure their conduct.

"He's softened some, don't you think?" J. T. asked me as we walked toward Spring Creek.

"I believe it's Nebo's doing," I replied. "Or maybe Pa's getting used to us again."

"Could be," J. T. agreed.

I actually enjoyed doing lessons at Mrs. Price's place. She wasn't half as severe as the teachers we'd had in town. When the weather was good, we studied outside, in the shade of several willow trees. She always sent us off to enjoy a midday swim, and she allowed Matt and me to choose most of our readings from a shelf of books borrowed from Colonel Stone.

"It's less important what you read than that you do read," she told us. "Besides, I know you two. You'd only prove a bother if I forced you to stomach some flowery poems or nonsense about some fool's old aunt."

I chose adventures with knights and dragons. Matt

picked stories by Mark Twain and Charles Dickens. I offered Nebo the loan of one of Twain's books about the Mississippi, but he declined.

"Better I don't think on those times too often," he explained. "The nightmares'll return."

I didn't know for certain how much schooling Nebo had. He was barely two years older than me, but he'd been with the army from '62 on. He liked ciphering, and he could read and write well enough.

"My pa was a cotton factor," Nebo told us one afternoon while helping Jamie and Ben with their addition. "Bought and sold cotton."

"I guess you were planning to be one, too, huh?" J. T. asked.

"No, I wanted to go to sea. I worked on a riverboat the summer the war started. Then the Yankee navy closed the river, and I joined our army. I'd still like to be a sailor, but the doctors told me I'd never last in a damp climate. One of my lungs is too weak."

"You don't have to worry too much about being wet here," I said, laughing. "Not unless you jump into the river."

"Hasn't yet," Jamie said. "You ought to start joining us for our midday swim, Nebo."

"A man has to earn his keep sometime," Nebo insisted. "Frank and I work during the day, you know."

I did know. First they built a rail fence around the house. Then they added a small room off the back of the house. I knew Pa had in mind we four boys could split up, but I suggested Nebo take the room.

"A body shouldn't have to pass the winter in a barn," I argued.

Ma decided I had a point, but she deemed four boys

too many for a single room. She moved Jamie and Ben into the new room and had Nebo shift his things in with J. T. and me.

"I'm still prone to nightmares," Nebo warned.

"We're used to Pa's hollering," J. T. replied. "We can abide yours."

In truth we tolerated Nebo just fine. It still bothered me some that Pa confided in him more than the rest of us, but I didn't see that changing. I tried not to think on it too much.

Sharing the creek and even our room with Nebo failed to prepare me for what happened at the harvest dance. It was a big to-do we generally held at Colonel Stone's place. We hadn't had one since '61. Too many husbands had marched off to war, I suppose. The colonel announced its revival, though, and people flocked from all over the county to his big hay barn. Boys generally invited girls, of which there was a shortage along Spring Creek. I invited Maureen.

"You're a day late," she said. "Besides, you're too close a relative. I'm going with Nebo Hill."

"Nebo?" I asked. "I'll bet he's got two left feet. You and I always go together."

"Well, we don't swim together anymore, remember? A girl wants a better time than dancing with her cousin."

"You remember I invited you," I scolded her. "When Nebo bruises your feet or swings you into the punch bowl, don't blame me."

"I won't," she promised. "Meanwhile, why don't you and Matt invite the Hester twins. They're nice enough, and they won't expect too much."

"That what we are, not too much?"

"Afraid so," she answered. "Ask quick before J. T. and Jamie beat you to it."

Since the Hesters attended Mrs. Price's school, we spoke to them the very next day.

"We'd be pleased to come, Albert," Marie, the prettier twin, told me. "We'll have to leave at sundown, though. Pa doesn't allow frivolous conduct after dark."

That didn't leave much time for dancing, since we didn't start eating until after six. It was less of a problem than I supposed because the Hesters didn't know so much as a two-step. As for Nebo, I couldn't have been more amazed about anything. Looking at him, dressed in some of Pa's old trousers and a faded gingham shirt, you wouldn't expect much. He danced like a regular dandy, though. And later he surprised everyone by taking a turn at the fiddle.

"Bugle's not the only thing I can play," he boasted afterward.

It rankled me some to see him having so much fun with Maureen.

"I'm asking Maureen next year," Matt declared after the Hesters left with their pa. "She puts all the others to shame."

"Yeah," I agreed. "Who would have imagined it?"

When we finally started home that night, we were a sight. Uncle Mitch had Grandpa's wagon, and we youngsters piled in back with our cousins and half a dozen neighbors. It was too crowded for my liking, so Matt and I followed on foot. It gave me a chance to see just how well Nebo got along with my brothers.

It's a hard thing to realize you're not needed, but I saw for myself the truth of it. Everyone was just as happy without me.

47

"I've been thinking, Matt," I said as we hurried to keep pace. "Maybe Mr. Thurman's got work for somebody up in Sherman."

"I thought you were happy at school," Matt said.

"Reading another adventure won't make me any smarter," I argued. "I can keep accounts and stock shelves. There's got to be a need somewhere for that sort of fellow."

"You can't get rich keeping accounts," Matt said. "Your grandpa could tell you that. No, the real money hereabouts is in stock. My pa made a fortune driving cows into Kansas before the war, remember? Somebody's sure to organize a herd soon."

"A cowboy needs a horse," I pointed out.

"The drive provides the mounts," Matt explained. "I'll start asking around if you want me to."

"I do."

"Might be next year before anybody's interested, Alby. Got another idea?"

"Not yet," I said, "but let me think on it."

That Sunday being one of those when Reverend Paul Keller conducted services at Spring Creek, almost everyone who lived along the creek gathered to worship. Afterward we all ate together. It was a sobering occasion for Pa, as he could see for himself how desperate people had become. I don't think there were three good pairs of shoes among the congregation, and most of the children had a patch or two on their shirts and trousers. I saw him talking with the reverend for the better part of an hour. He sat for a time with Mrs. Price, too.

Pa changed that Sunday. Almost immediately he spoke with a softer voice. He found time to share a fable with Ben, and he didn't yell at me once. The next morning, as I collected my brothers for school, he suggested I stay at home.

"We've had a real scarcity of meat in this house," he said.

"I know," I said. "Pa, we—"

"It's not your doing, Alby," he told me. "But maybe you can help remedy the situation. Nebo said he spied some turkeys down by the creek yesterday. Let's see if we can shoot one or two."

"You want me to come along?"

"It's been a while since we went hunting," he said, gripping my shoulder. "Maybe, well, we can put right a thing or two."

I nodded. I remembered those days when I'd go along to shoot squirrels or rabbits. They were fine times.

"I'll get the rifle," I told him.

"Not quite yet," he cautioned. "Best to wait until the children have a chance to get to Miz Price's school. It's turkeys we're after, not schoolboys."

We waited close to an hour. When we did set off, I was surprised to find Nebo staying behind.

"He's got his chores," Pa explained. "I suspect we can manage without his chattering, too."

"Oh?" I asked. Most of the time Nebo spent words like they were silver dollars. Except for our talk at the creek, I couldn't recall him gabbing more than a minute or so since arriving.

"Be best to leave the dog behind, too," Pa said. I tied Splinter to one of the porch posts.

Pa had a difficult time making his way to the creek. The crutch was awkward at the best of times, and the rough, uneven ground posed a menace. I carried his rifle and a cowhide game bag. I handed him the gun when we stopped deep in a nest of hackberries and briers.

"Tough going," he said as he eased himself to the ground behind a fallen blackjack oak. "Puts me in mind of that ground north of Murfreesboro where the Ninth broke the Yankee line."

"Must've been hard, fighting in such country."

"It's hard fighting most times," he told me. "Well, the killing anyway. Losing friends."

"Matt's pa," I said, sighing.

"Hundreds of others. Wasn't so bad in the beginning, when we believed there was some purpose to it. Later, after we saw how the people were suffering, I couldn't find much use in it."

"Why'd you go on?"

"Suppose it was easier to keep at it than to stop. Pure mule stubbornness, I guess. Well, the Yanks kept going, too, and they were bleeding same as us."

I swallowed hard and searched the ground ahead for tracks. It wasn't long afterward that Pa began making turkey calls. Soon a big gobbler peeked out of the briers fifty feet to our left.

"Just like Shiloh," Pa whispered as he loaded his rifle. His hands trembled, and his face flooded with pain. "No, Chickamauga."

"You said Murfreesboro," I told him.

"It was," he said, coughing. The turkey raced away, and Pa slapped the ground.

"There'll be another," I assured him.

"Always is," he said as he fumbled with a percussion cap. It was just a little piece of copper and explosive, but you needed it to spark the powder. It fit on a knob in front of the hammer. Pa couldn't manage it. Finally he passed me the rifle.

"You know how to shoot, don't you?" he asked as I placed the hammer at half cock and affixed the cap.

"Yes, sir," I answered. "I'm not so worthless as you might think."

"Never said— Well, I never meant it, anyhow," he said, pointing to where the turkey was reemerging from the thicket. "Take your time, son. Don't hurry the shot."

I balanced the rifle, drew the hammer back to full cock, and took aim. It was a simple enough matter, but I dreaded the notion of a missed shot. I waited until the bird was in clear view. Then I took a deep breath, let it go, and fired. The concussion shattered the silence of the thicket. Birds cried in alarm, and leaves cascaded down from the trees overhead. My shot tore through the breast of the turkey, and it fell dead on the spot.

"Wait a moment," Pa said, pushing me to the ground when I started to rise and fetch the carcass. "Don't you hear them?"

"Hear what?" I asked, confused.

"The drums. They're coming. Hurry, boy, load your rifle. You have to be ready for 'em."

I started to object, but he tore the rifle from my hands and hurriedly reloaded. I'd never seen him work so fast. He barely got the ramrod out of the barrel before swinging the rifle toward the thicket and firing. There was nothing but a cloud of powder smoke.

"Pa?" I asked.

"Cap!" he shouted. "Give me a cap!"

"Only brought two," I explained. "We're short—"

"Where's my bayonet?" he cried, shoving the rifle into my hands. "Lord, boys, they're coming!"

He tried to get to his feet, but his leg failed him, and he collapsed. "Run, Nebo!" he screamed. "Leave me."

"Nebo's not here, Pa," I said, shaking his shoulder. "Pa, it's me, Alby!"

He got to his feet and began shouting commands. He screamed at trees and rocks, talking to them like they were soldiers. He was still carrying on when Nebo arrived.

"Nebo, he's gone crazy," I warned.

"I feared he would do this," Nebo said, stepping to Pa's side. The bugler whispered something, and Pa became quiet.

"Is he all right?" I asked.

"Mostly," Nebo told me. "Fetch your turkey, Alby. I'd best get Frank home."

"I could . . ." I began. The crazed look in Pa's eyes persuaded me to do as instructed. I shouldered the rifle and started toward the turkey. "At least we'll have meat," I told myself. It was poor consolation for witnessing a nightmare.

Pa didn't say much about the hunt, and I couldn't. I was too unsettled. I wanted to talk about it with somebody, but I didn't know who to turn to. Ma would be troubled over the notion of Pa gone addled, and it would upset my brothers even more. I kept my thoughts to myself.

In the end, it was Maureen who noticed.

"You're not yourself," she told me when I returned to school.

"Who would want to be me?" I asked.

"You don't have it so hard," she scolded. "There are four of you and Nebo besides to spread the chores among. Eben and I just have each other."

"Well, you've got a whole pa," I argued.

Maureen paled.

"I never thought I'd hear such a thing from you, Alby Draper," she declared. "Half a pa? Why, Matt would trade you in an instant. Half a pa? A man doesn't need both his legs to be useful."

"It's not his leg that's the trouble," I said, taking her aside. "It's—"

"Oh," she said, nodding. "It's that."

"What?" I asked.

"Nightmares. Well, not exactly nightmares. More like nightmares when you're wide awake."

"He told you?"

"Nobody had to tell me," she said. "You're not the only one whose pa went to war."

"Uncle Mitch?"

"He's gotten better, Alby. Wait and see if Uncle Frank doesn't, too."

"He scared me."

"I know," she said, resting her head against my shoulder. "One morning Eben went to rouse Pa. It was raining, and a big flash of lightning hit an oak tree outside. Pa woke with a start, grabbed Eben, and halfway smothered him before Ma and I could pry him loose."

"What can we do?"

"Hope it passes," Maureen suggested. "Pray a lot. Ma and I do. Eben keeps to himself once the sun sets."

I knew how he felt.

I thought about going home with Maureen and Eben that afternoon. Maybe Uncle Mitch could explain it. Matt insisted I help him put some books away when school was over, though, and I lost the chance.

"You still looking for hire work?" he asked me after the others had gone.

"I am," I replied.

"You remember me mentioning the cattle drive my pa went on before the war?"

"A few times," I said, grinning. "I don't think Texans would be very welcome in Kansas just now."

"It's too late to start north anyway," he said.

"So what do you have in mind, Matt?"

"Some stock raisers plan to ride out west and hunt longhorns. You know Wise County's about deserted. They say you can collect a thousand head in a week's time."

"And do what with them?"

"Sell 'em to the Yankees."

"How?" I asked.

"They've got cavalry stationed at Jacksboro," Matt explained. "There's talk of putting up a fort there to fend off the Comanches. Soldiers have to eat, don't they?"

"Yankees would pay in greenbacks," I said. "We'd have money for taxes."

"And more besides," he observed. "Alby, it would be an adventure, getting away for a time, riding horses—"

"Horses?"

"Any man who goes along gets a pony," Matt told me. "That's worth the trip. We also get a share of the profits."

"Men, you said. Matt, even stretching ourselves, we hardly pass for men."

"You see many taller hereabouts?" he asked. "They'll need bodies to do this job, and we're handy."

"So how do we manage it?"

"You doing anything special?"

"Now?" I asked. "I don't even have lessons to do tonight. Where do we go?"

"Colonel Stone's," Matt said. "Let's hurry. Once word spreads, every boy for fifty miles around will be headed there."

I wasn't all that hopeful myself, but when we arrived

at the Stone place, things were pretty much as Matt told me. Major Ben Keller, who rode with John Hunt Morgan's Confederate raiders during the war, was in charge. Everybody in northern Texas knew of him. He'd planned to be a preacher, like his pa, but he'd joined the cavalry instead. After Morgan was killed, the major continued to plague the Yankees. Some said he was more ghost than soldier, but he was real enough. I shook his hand.

"I'm Albert Sidney Johnston Draper," I announced.

"Named for the hero of Shiloh," Major Keller said, smiling. "Your ma must've had foresight. You appear a hair old to've been named for the late general."

"Pa served with him in Mexico," I explained. "Pa was with the Ninth Texas Infantry more recently."

"Good batch of boys," Colonel Stone said, joining us. "How's Frank doing, Alby?"

"Not so well," I said, avoiding his eyes. "Leg's troubling him some."

"Many's the man with reminders of the war," Major Keller said, raising his left hand. The last two fingers were gone.

"I'm Matt Price," Matt told them. "We neither of us have ponies, Major, but we're hard workers."

"Can you ride?" Major Keller asked.

"I carried the mail to Sherman and back two years," I boasted.

"Ma says I must've been born on horseback," Matt added. "I rode regular until the quartermasters took my horse."

"We'll have to make that right," Colonel Stone declared. "Come over and show us, boys. Our stock's somewhat raw, but you stay atop, we'll take you along."

Raw was an understatement. The colonel had a

handful of half-wild mustangs. I had a fight of it just getting mine saddled. As for staying mounted, well, we each had our own notions on that score.

"Easy, boy," I whispered each time I prepared to mount. "It's just me, Alby." I gave that pony an apple one time. The next time I gave him a little sugar coaxed off Mrs. Stone. Whether it was that, or the poor animal got tired of throwing me, I'll never know. I was soon riding, though.

Matt used a different method. Whenever his horse began bucking, he hugged its neck and bit one ear.

"He feels that ear, he quits worrying about the weight on his back," Matt said, spitting the taste out of his mouth.

"I couldn't do that," I told him later that afternoon. "Horses and me, we're of a kind, Grandpa says. I couldn't hurt one."

"You get a rank horse, you need more than your smile to get you on top," Matt said, pointing to the men sitting on the top rail of the corral fence. "See those spurs? They're not for looks. You saw that fellow with the whip, too."

"I saw it," I said, frowning. "Didn't like it much."

"Biting an ear just lets the horse know who he's got on top of him," Matt argued.

"And who'd that be? A beaver?"

Matt couldn't help laughing. I tossed a dirt clod at him, and we ended up chasing each other around the corral half an hour. By then the sun was starting to set, and I prepared to head home.

"We leave at daybreak, boys," Colonel Stone told us. "Don't be late."

"Tomorrow?" I asked.

"I know you don't have much time to convince

Amanda," the colonel said, nodding gravely. "But there's good money in this enterprise. Tell her I promise to keep an eye on you."

Actually, though, it wasn't Ma who needed convincing. She was used to me riding to Sherman, after all. Or maybe she just knew how badly we needed the money.

"It's plain foolishness," Pa argued. "Alby, what about your lessons?"

"Matt's going," I countered. "His ma will see we both catch up."

"It's better than a hundred miles to Jacksboro," Pa pointed out. "Rivers and creeks between here and there that can drown you."

"I swim well, Pa," I assured him.

"Son, there are Comanches riding all over that country," Pa continued. "Why do you think those cattle are out there running free? A hundred men wouldn't be safe."

"We don't plan on fighting them, Pa. If we have to, we'll get by. Major Keller's in charge, and he rode with Morgan's cavalry. They ran the Yankees all over Kentucky and even invaded Ohio!"

"Morgan's dead, Alby," Pa reminded me. "Moreover, no Yankee that ever lived held a candle to a Comanche."

"Do you know any better way to make some money?" I asked. "I get a horse and a share of the profits. Colonel Stone judges that's twenty dollars maybe. Enough to pay the tax bill, don't you think?"

"Might be," Ma agreed. Pa started to object, but she hushed him with a glance. "I don't suppose we've got many alternatives, Alby, but I don't want to hear of you taking chances. Follow your orders, and stay close to the colonel."

"He promised to keep an eye on Matt and me," I told her.

"He knows he daren't do otherwise," she said, nodding as if to emphasize the point. "Get plenty of rest tonight."

"Do your best," Pa added. "You've been promised fair payment, so deliver an honest day's work."

I wanted to boast that I'd never done otherwise, but I was afraid he might argue the point. I didn't want to hear that, so I kept mum.

Matt and I arrived at Colonel Stone's at first light that next morning. A handful of men were already there. Most were wild-eyed fellows wearing the ragged remains of Confederate uniforms. Two of the men rode horses with U.S. branded on their rumps.

"I'm certain that you came by those animals honestly, boys," Major Keller said, "but as we're doing business with the Yankee cavalry, you might want to leave your horses and ride one of mine."

We all had a good laugh at that. Major Keller, during his army days, was famous for taking his enemy's horses.

"You youngsters ride with old Bowl there," the major told Matt and me. "Old" Bowl was Henry Bowling of Sherman. He was all of seventeen and not an inch taller than I was. I knew his ma from my mail rider days.

"Sure, I know you," he said, smiling in that easy way some Texans have that seems to light their whole face. "Your pa ever make it home?"

"Yes," I answered nervously.

"Mine died at Chickamauga," Matt volunteered.

"I was there," Henry said, sighing. "Hard place, that one. Good thing I was a little fellow. They shot my hat four times!"

He laughed, and I couldn't help smiling. It was about the last cause for us to do either for better than a week.

As it turned out, we didn't have any Comanche trouble. No, and we didn't enjoy much luck, either. There were plenty of stray cattle in Wise County, and even more between there and Jacksboro. The trouble was collecting them. None of us was any too skilled where working cattle was concerned, and our horses spooked at the first sight of those long, deadly-looking horns. Matt and I did as well as most, but that wasn't very well at all. Henry tried to use a rope's end to persuade a big bull to move along, missed, and had his horse gored.

After several trials and plenty of mistakes, we finally formed a line and drove the cattle westward. We didn't actually control them. We simply made it easier to go that way than any other. In the end we coaxed two hundred head into Jacksboro, only to discover that the army wasn't buying beef. At least not from Texans.

"You need to talk to the quartermasters," a youngish lieutenant told Major Keller. "Now if you'd care to sell your horses, we could arrange something."

A couple of the men agreed to turn their ponies over, but the cavalry didn't want raw mustangs.

"They require breaking," a scar-faced sergeant growled when he looked the ponies over. "Work 'em some and come back. I can't put a recruit on a wild animal."

Colonel Stone and Major Keller called us together and shared the sour news.

"I know you were all expecting something more,"

the colonel said. "So was I. I promised you each a horse, and I can manage that. Ben and I will bear the cost. You take your mounts and as many cattle as you care to drive home. Some of that stock looks promising. You'd at least have beef to eat all winter."

It was discouraging news, all right, but Matt and I took it better than most. We chose twenty head and started home with them.

Now I don't know what made us think we could manage those cows any better on our own than with the others. Matt recalled his pa's tales of trailing cattle to Kansas, and he was sure he could keep them calm by singing. That might have worked better a few months before. Lately his voice was all squeaks and squawks. The cows didn't take to either.

It got worse quickly. The second night out of Jacksboro the sky darkened, and lightning flashed overhead. Almost instantly the cattle stirred.

"Matt?" I called.

"Pa never talked about what to do in a storm," he told me.

"Then I think we'd better find a place to hide," I said.

We tied our horses to locust trees and hoped their thorny branches would discourage the longhorns from heading that way. They did, but that didn't stop the cows from running in every other direction imaginable the first chance they got. The ground shook, first with thunder and then with stampeding hooves. Matt and I huddled behind some rocks and watched in terror as our little herd pounded the ground ten yards away.

It was bad enough losing the cows, but the storm didn't stop at that. It came at us with rare fury, tearing

61

at our clothes, flinging branches, scattering our blankets and only cook pot. In the end, our ponies broke away, too. We were the better part of a day finding them, and we recovered only three of the cows.

Bad as we felt, I feared we had additional trials to face. We remained seventy miles from home. We had nothing to eat. We passed a whole morning sewing pieces of torn shirts onto our frayed britches so we wouldn't embarrass ourselves upon meeting strangers on the road.

Actually, strangers provided us at least one bit of fun. We were riding along the remains of the old Fort Belknap military road when a pair of men with flour sacks over their faces stopped us.

"Give us your money!" one of them ordered.

I dropped my face in my hands and began laughing. Matt, who had the good sense to be afraid, pleaded that we had no money.

"Look at us," he urged. "We're close to naked. We've got three cows you can take if you can convince 'em to follow you."

"What's so funny?" the second outlaw demanded.

I just looked at him and sighed.

"We can't even get robbed proper," I said.

"I believe these boys are worse off than us," the first stranger said. Pretty soon they were laughing loudest of all. In the end they shared some jerked beef and rode on.

We were almost home when the second storm hit. It was every bit as bad as the first, and we rode with abandon along the Preston road, hoping to find refuge. Eventually I spied the shell of a shed, and we weathered the worst of the storm under what was left of its roof. Our three cows ran off, but the ponies found shelter close by, and we located them come daybreak.

We tramped the last few miles along Spring Creek as disheartened as two boys ever were. Mud spatters covered our ponies and caked our legs to the knees. I had burrs in my hair, blisters on my hands, and scratches and scrapes on nearly every inch of me.

"We could stop by Colonel Stone's place and pick up some food," Matt suggested.

"I only want to get home," I told him.

"Me, too," he agreed.

We finally parted company, and I rode the last hundred yards half asleep. Ben spotted me first, and he ran toward the house as if ten devils were chasing him. Ma appeared, shotgun in hand, but once she realized that it was me, she started laughing.

"You're a sight, Alby!" J. T. hollered from the barn.

"That can't be Alby," Ben argued.

"Afraid so," I said.

"You didn't fare too well," Ma observed. "Did you make it to Jacksboro?"

"We drove two hundred head there," I answered. "Cavalry wasn't buying. I meant to bring ten back here, but I got caught in a storm. The cows ran off."

"You didn't get the money then?" Ma asked, not angrily but with terrible disappointment.

"I even lost the cook pot you loaned me," I said, staring at the ground. "I got this horse, but that's all."

"Well, you tried," she said, forcing a smile onto her face.

"That doesn't mean much, Ma," I said. "I can't imagine where we'll get the tax money."

"Nor can I," she said sadly.

I dreaded Pa's response to my failure. He'd warned me of trouble, hadn't he? He'd been right, and I expected him to remind me of it. Instead, he said nothing. I read the disappointment in his eyes, though.

Ma insisted that I clean up before coming inside the house, so I walked to the barn. J. T. helped me roll out the wooden bathtub, and Ma heated water. After J. T. and I emptied three buckets of well water into the tub, Nebo arrived with a steaming kettle.

"If I didn't know better, I'd guess that you'd been to war," he told me.

"Have, in a way," I said, peeling the ragged remnant of my shirt off my back. "A few scratches, but no scars. So I guess it wasn't really a war."

"Maybe not," J. T. said, "but you sure are muddy!"

I couldn't dispute that. I slid out of my tattered overalls and stepped into the tub. Instantly the clear water turned to muck, and I had to do some real scrubbing to make myself presentable. Once I did, I squeezed myself into an old pair of trousers and buttoned on one of Pa's shirts. I looked like a scarecrow! It might have been funny if I'd had anything better to wear.

"You forgot something, didn't you?" Pa called from the door.

"I don't know what," I answered.

"Those scratches need tending," Pa said. "Sit down on that bench there and strip off the shirt. It won't take long."

I did as told, and he stirred a tin of reddish brown paste.

"Don't worry, Alby," Pa said as he painted each scratch. "I've had a lot of practice."

"During the war?" I asked.

"During the wars," he explained. "We had a surgeon in Mexico who couldn't tell an arm from a peach pit. I was only a corporal, but my grandma taught me cures for everything from stomach gripe to swamp fever. I got in the habit of doctoring, and I kept at it."

"I don't remember you doing any doctoring, Pa," J. T. said, joining me on the bench.

"Doc Crawford's just an hour's ride away," Pa pointed out. "I trust him to tend the sick hereabouts. Just didn't figure to bother him over a few scratches."

Pa went on dabbing his ointment. When he finished, he had me wait for it to dry. Only then did I put on my shirt. J. T. and I dragged the tub out of the barn and dumped the muddy water.

When we approached the house, I could smell ham baking in the oven.

"We butchered a hog just for you, Alby," Jamie told me. "Wish it was a cow. We could eat off that for a week."

"Maybe we'll drive some cows down later," I said,

mussing his hair. "I saw a few of 'em out there, and we got three as far as the Preston road."

"That's not far from here," J. T. declared. "I'll bet we could head out there tomorrow."

"You've got school tomorrow," Pa reminded us.

"Sure," J. T. said, mumbling something to himself. Before Pa had a chance to chide him, a wagon rumbled up from the creek. We all stared with some measure of surprise when we recognized Mitchell French.

"Uncle Mitch's come to dinner!" Jamie exclaimed.

"What?" Ma asked.

"Heard Alby'd gotten home," Mitch said, waving me to the wagon. "Got a question or two for him."

"After we eat," Ma insisted. "Wash yourself, Mitchell. Then come join us."

Uncle Mitch appeared reluctant, but when the wind blew his way, he got a whiff of baked ham. He headed right to the well, drew a bucket of spring water, and dumped it over his dusty face. He happily shared our dinner, and he didn't ask me a single question. Afterward he led the way to the porch and we sat down together.

"I was at the Stone place yesterday and heard all about it, Alby," he told me. "Poor market for cows, huh? Well, we'll bring some down before winter comes. Should help fill out the brothers, and you can tan the hides. Craft shoes out of them."

"We didn't have much luck herding those cows," I said.

"I'll teach you the art of it," he promised. "Tell me, though. What route did you travel coming home?"

"We followed the Elm Fork of the Trinity most of the way," I explained. "Then we cut across some low hills."

66

"After that you saw a plain cut by a creek or two, but mostly flat?"

"High grass," I said, remembering it. "A few longhorns grazed here and there, but mostly I remember horse tracks. Maybe a party of Comanches rode through."

"No, the tracks would have been shallow. The ponies weren't carrying the weight of riders."

"No, they weren't," I realized.

"That's Mustang Flats," Uncle Mitch announced. "Good horse-hunting country."

"What?"

"I talked to Colonel Stone. He said the soldiers offered to buy horses."

"We'd have to gentle them first," I said. "They refused to buy raw stock."

"Frank," Uncle Mitch called. "You remember the Flats?"

"Mustang Flats?" he asked. A brightness filled his eyes for a second, and he nearly smiled. "That was a long time ago."

"Not so long," Uncle Mitch argued. "Remember how we used to ride out there and rope a mustang or two?"

"I was a whole man then," Pa grumbled. "Younger, too."

"I'm not saying it'll be easy, Frank, but the colonel said the cavalry's paying forty dollars a head minimum for horses. Good mounts go even higher."

"We could earn the tax money pretty quickly," I said. "Just capture a handful and break them to the saddle."

"You'd know all about that, would you, son?" Pa asked. "Like you knew all about rounding up cows?"

"We got the cows," I replied. "Nobody wanted to buy them. They wanted horses, Pa. I heard the soldiers say so."

"Can't manage it, Mitch," Pa said, shaking his head. "We had our share of trouble before, and both of us were young and full of beans. These boys, well, it just won't work."

Pa marched off past the well, and I sighed.

"It was a fine notion," I told Uncle Mitch.

"Don't be so quick to give up on it," Uncle Mitch counseled. "The thing is, Alby, a man misses a leg a lot less when he's mounted. You wouldn't remember, but your pa's about the best fellow with a rope I've ever seen. He could throw a loop over a steam locomotive and bring it to a stop. He's got a way with horses, too. If we roped half a dozen, we could gentle them and collect payment before the taxes are due."

"If we don't have the money, they can take the farm, can't they?"

"Yes, son, that's the heart of the matter. We can't allow it."

"But there's more to it."

"Alby, Maureen's told me about your hunt. A man never entirely escapes what we've been through, but if he hasn't got any purpose to his days, it's worse. The war took more than Frank's leg. It robbed him of his heart. We have to find a way to get it back for him or I'm afraid all this anger's going to eat him up."

"And hunting horses will make him different?"

"See if it doesn't," Uncle Mitch said, pointing to where Pa and Nebo stood, talking. "Come on. Let's have another try at him."

Uncle Mitch and I walked together to the well. When we got close, Pa stopped talking and turned toward us. His face reddened some, and he tapped his fingers nervously on the stone walls of the well.

"You ever see this boy ride, Frank?" Uncle Mitch asked.

"I've seen him spatter mud," Pa answered.

"He's just like you on a horse, Frank," Uncle Mitch said, resting his hand on my right shoulder. "Even without a proper saddle, you can tell he's a born rider. We could have used him in the cavalry."

"No!" Pa shouted.

"John Tyler should come, too. Open country's good for an inch of growth. Matt Price would want to join us. Young Nebo here, too. What do you say?"

"I've said it about every way I know," Pa growled. "No!"

"That's the wrong answer, Pa," I told him. "Ask Ma if there's another way to earn the tax money. I don't know one. You wouldn't have to do more than your leg'll allow. The rest of us can help. Can't you see, though? We've got to try."

"He's right, Frank," Uncle Mitch said.

"Alby, it's a fool's errand," Pa declared. "Won't be my first, though."

"Then we'll have a go at it?"

"Well, this country's been trying to kill me since '51," Pa said, shaking his head. "Guess it's due another chance."

J. T. let out a whoop and tossed his hat in the air. It roused Splinter from his early evening nap, and the collie raced over and began licking my fingers.

"We're going horse hunting, boy," I said, scratching

69

behind Splinter's ears the way he liked. "We won't be losing this place after all."

"That's far from certain," Pa cautioned.

I didn't believe him. When everyone else gave up, we believed he'd come home. It just made no sense that he'd come back so we could lose our home!

It took better than a week to ready ourselves for the horse hunt. Pa was determined that we would have every chance of success, and he reminded me continually how ill-prepared Colonel Stone had been to take on two hundred cattle. Uncle Mitch and I scouted Mustang Flats, making certain there were ponies up that way. We never got very close, but we saw plenty of flying hooves and dancing tails.

"They're none too friendly," Uncle Mitch observed.

"Well, maybe they know what we've got in mind," I said. "I remember what a battle Ma had when she sent me off to school the first time. Nobody gives up his free ways without a fight."

"Sure," Uncle Mitch admitted. "Guess that's true enough."

On our way back we collected seven stray cows. I thought Uncle Mitch probably just wanted some stock at hand to provide for our families, but that wasn't it at all. We no sooner returned than he loaded a pistol and shot the first animal dead.

"Get the knives, Alby," Pa told me. "Time you learned how to butcher a beeve."

"But Pa—"

"I need the hide and some of the horn," he said. "The hooves for making glue. Be a shame to waste the meat, though. We'll smoke it, salt it proper, and cut it into jerky strips."

"Yes, sir," I said, turning to fetch the knives. Ma already had them out.

"Pay attention," she urged. "It isn't very pleasant, Alby, but you'll need to do it yourself one day."

I nodded. It wasn't that I'd never dressed meat before, but we hadn't had cattle on the farm since '62. The way Pa worked, nearly every piece of that cow was usable for something. J. T. rode my pony down Spring Creek and summoned neighbors. Pa offered meat to anyone who asked. We smoked and jerked the rest.

It was, as Pa had said, the hides he was after. He cut every scrap of meat from each one. Then he stretched and dried it. Next he soaked oak bark in buckets. Finally he dipped the hides in the liquid. They became hard but pliable.

"Now I'll teach you a genuine Texas art," Pa said.

The only real saddle I'd ever sat on belonged to Grandpa French. He brought it out so Pa could use it as a model.

"I've never made a Texas saddle before," Pa said. "It suits our work better than the sort I've seen in the army. See how you've got a good strong horn to tie your rope to? And look at all the places you can carry things."

Pa was good at copying, and he used the better part of each hide to make a saddle. Ma, Aunt Lottie, and Maureen did most of the sewing. I cut the pieces after Pa marked them out.

Once everyone else was busy making saddles, Pa cut rawhide strips and began weaving lariats.

"You won't hold a good pony with a rope," Pa said. "Not the kind you can buy these days. Besides, rope has a bad habit of tearing and burning flesh. It's hard to throw, too."

"If you don't use a rope, why call it roping?" J. T. asked.

"Son, if you start trying to make sense out of such things, you'll go crazy in a week," Grandpa declared. "Just watch and learn. In forty years or so your own grandchildren will ask the same questions. Maybe you'll figure it out for them."

"You haven't," J. T. grumbled.

"Complain to me, then," Grandpa said, laughing.

We managed most of our needs without asking for help, but we had one big problem. As I'd told Matt weeks before, you couldn't throw a loop over a mustang unless he was mounted. Matt and I had our mustangs. Uncle Mitch borrowed Grandpa's gray, and we had a pair of mules to haul the wagon. Pa had no mount, and neither did J. T. We all figured Pa might drive the wagon, but Nebo deemed himself best suited for that task.

"You could borrow two horses from Colonel Stone," Ma suggested.

"A man makes his own way," Pa insisted.

"Sometimes he's got no choice but to ask for help," Ma argued. "Frank, can't you see the truth of it?"

"I won't be beholden to the Stones," he vowed. "You know as well as I do how the colonel operates. We'll end up promising him our horses, and he'll see all the profit."

73

"You have to catch a horse before you can sell him," Ma pointed out.

As it happened, though, Pa's generosity with the meat solved his problem. Jack Hester offered the loan of two good saddle ponies.

"I'll need 'em back, of course," Mr. Hester told Pa.

"I don't feel right, borrowing off a neighbor," Pa replied.

"We're neighbors, Frank, but considering the way my girls eye your Alby, we might be family in a few years."

That may have improved Pa's view of things, but it did nothing for mine. Pretty little Marie had gone plump, and her twin, Abigail, stayed up nights sharpening her tongue.

We finally set out for Mustang Flats the middle of October. By then the nights were cool and the skies prone to cloud over and pelt us with rain or hail. Days were short, too. I wished we could have done our horse hunting earlier, under a warming sun. Tax bills were out, though, and ours came to thirty-seven dollars. We had until November first to arrange payment.

Mustang Flats formed the southeast corner of Denton County. It was good land, and a few farmers had plowed sections here and there. Most of it remained wild country, though. There were several decent-sized creeks to water stock, and low hills broke the monotony of the landscape. It took us the better part of a whole day to get there, and we had left before dawn. The air was cold by the time Nebo halted the wagon near a sheltering grove of live oaks.

"It's as good a place as the next," he said. "If you fellows will let my mules out of their harness, I'll get a fire started and cook us some dinner."

That suited me, so Matt and I volunteered to tend the mules. We released them from their harness and tied hobbles around their feet to keep them from straying. It was pretty much the same thing we did to our ponies. We left the stock to drink from a pond formed by a free-flowing spring. They could graze in the nearby pasture.

While Nebo prepared dinner, Pa and Uncle Mitch stretched a sheet of canvas between two trees and made us a shelter. It wouldn't protect us much from a real storm, but it would keep raindrops off. Pa explained how that was about all the cover they'd had in the war.

"We'd build huts if we stayed in one place long enough, but whenever you got fixed up proper, some general was sure to move you halfway across the state."

Uncle Mitch started in with a soldier recollection of his own then, and I led Matt down to the pond. We drank our fill of the icy, fresh water. It seemed to bring me back to life after a day of stirring up dust. I washed my face and neck with a wet kerchief. Then we filled a bucket with water for Nebo.

Later we went back down there and soaked our feet. My birthday moccasins were a poor substitute for boots, and I wished Pa could have crafted me something better from a cowhide.

"When we finish with the mustangs, we'll run some cows back home," Pa promised. "We'll have hides enough for shoes then."

I couldn't really complain, though. When J. T. joined us, I saw how scratched and torn his bare feet had become.

"You'd better wrap them in cloth tomorrow," I advised. "Maybe we can tear up a blanket."

"We don't have enough blankets now," J. T. argued. "I'll live."

When he dipped his feet in the pond, though, he let out a loud yelp and jumped clear.

"Something stabbed me!" he cried.

Sure enough, his right foot was bleeding. I eased my way over and felt the rocky bottom with my fingers. I touched something flat and sharp. After a moment of tugging and prying, I freed a sharp sliver of stone.

"Look there," Matt said, hopping over. "An arrowhead."

"Is it really?" J. T. asked. "Give it to me. I want to show Pa."

I handed over the arrowhead. J. T. forgot about his pain as he announced our discovery. Nebo silenced the noise with his own call.

"Dinner's waiting!" he shouted.

Matt and I concluded our foot-soaking and returned to camp. We each accepted a plate of salted beef and potatoes, topped off with some wild onions. For once there was plenty to eat, and even the growing chill of the air failed to cool our spirits.

After eating, Pa drew us to the fire and fingered J. T.'s arrowhead.

"There was a time," he began, "when only Indians and buffalo knew this country. No one had ever heard of Stephen Austin or Texas. At least not the state. It was just a Caddo word for 'friend' back then. I guess

76

they gave it to the white men they met, hoping they would be good neighbors."

"Don't suppose they were," Matt said, shivering. "I haven't seen any Caddos hereabouts."

"You figure the Caddos left that here, Pa?" J. T. asked.

"No, it's newer'n that, son." Pa looked closer at the arrowhead. "More likely Comanche or Kiowa. During the war some of their raiding parties passed just north and west of here. A few might have come through the flats hunting horses, just like we're doing now."

"What are they like, Comanches?" Matt asked.

"Most folks are scared of 'em," J. T. noted.

"Should be," Pa said, staring into the fire. "They're fierce fighters. I had a brush with them once just after returning from fighting down in Mexico. I don't think they're very different as men. They fight to protect their wives and children. I never sat down and spoke with one, but I don't figure he wants much more than I do. To protect those who are in his care. Besides that, he probably wants to be left alone."

"But Pa fought 'em," I boasted.

"Mostly they fought us," Pa explained. "I was camped with some of my men out on the Brazos. A half dozen families, mostly German settlers, were across the way. Comanches rode down, hoping to steal some horses. When they saw us, they screamed to high heaven and attacked." He studied our wide eyes a moment before continuing. "They saw our soldier coats," Pa told us. "We were already discharged, but they didn't know it. We had rifles, and we formed a line. Before you could say Tuesday, we gave them a smart volley that emptied three saddles. The rest turned and ran."

"You killed three of them, then," Matt said, nodding soberly. "Good shooting."

"Not so good," Pa said. "We found only one body. Those other fellows got away. At the time I was angry, but now I'm not unhappy. Been enough killing lately."

"And enough tale spinning," Nebo declared. "Best we try and get some rest."

"Sure," I agreed, leading the way to the makeshift shelter. We dragged leaves over and made ourselves little nests on which to spread our blankets. Uncle Mitch and Pa slept on the far side, leaving Matt, J. T., and me to make our beds on the other side. Nebo slept in between.

At first I felt pretty snug under my blanket. The leaves kept the cold from the ground away for a time. Later, though, the wind picked up. I felt my toes turn to ice.

"Wish Splinter was here," J. T. whispered as he burrowed into the leaves beside me. "He'd sleep on our feet and keep 'em warm."

"I'm not sure even Splinter could manage that tonight," Matt grumbled.

The three of us huddled for warmth, but we just didn't have enough cover to shut out the cold.

"I miss the fire," J. T. complained. "Maybe we could drag our blankets over there."

"Nothing left but coals," Matt said, sneezing. "It's better'n this, though."

"Cold?" Nebo asked from his bed five feet away.

"Freezing," I answered.

He slipped out of his blanket and crawled over.

He'd stripped to his drawers, and I couldn't understand why he wasn't cold.

"First thing to do's shed all those clothes," he said. "You get to sweating, and later that turns to ice. Freezes you solid."

"Then what?" I asked.

"Build yourself a fireplace," he said, grinning. We didn't have any idea what he was talking about, so he showed us. He produced a bayonet and dug out a trench five inches or so below each of our beds. He then took a spade from the wagon and brought over a few glowing coals from the fire. He covered them with earth, saw to it the surface was just warm—not hot enough to ignite leaves—and rebuilt our little nests.

It was amazing. The ground wasn't hot exactly, but our beds provided a warmth I wouldn't have believed.

"Kept me from freezing my innards on many a chill Tennessee night," Nebo explained.

"Thanks, Nebo," I said.

"Yeah," J. T. said. "Thanks."

"You're more'n welcome, boys," Nebo replied. "Glad to come along."

I lay in my new warmth several minutes, feeling more content than I could remember. Then I heard Nebo cough.

"He shouldn't be out here in the cold," J. T. said. "It's damp, too. You know he's got a bad lung, Alby."

"He's had a hard road to travel," I observed. "Losing his family at Vicksburg. Getting shot to pieces."

"Did you see all those scars?" Matt asked.

"I don't think they trouble him half as much as the

79

ghosts of his ma and pa," I said, fighting an image of them from my mind.

"You're right," Matt assured us. "I dream of Pa all the time."

"Sure," I said, sighing. "We almost lost Pa."

"Maybe," J. T. added. "But I think we're getting him back."

That next morning I was the first to rise. It was still dark, but a noise attracted my attention. I wrapped my blanket around my shoulders and moved along past the smoldering remains of our fire. The air felt like a thousand cactus spines pricking every inch of me, and I shivered. Then, as the sun touched the eastern horizon with its first trace of yellow, I saw it.

"Now that's a horse," I said, gazing at what appeared only half animal and half apparition. It was black as the darkest midnight, more shadow than beast. Behind it for a hundred yards mares and colts spread out.

"It's Demon," Pa said as he crutched his way to my side. "Would you look at that! He's got thirty mares in his harem, and I can't begin to count all the colts and fillies."

"Must be a quarter of the horses in all of Texas," I said, rubbing my eyes. I half expected the ponies were only phantoms.

"That stallion's been running here since '58, maybe even before that," Pa told me. "Every spring he makes

81

his rounds, luring mares off the ranches. There's fifty dollars bounty on him, but no one's ever been able to put a bullet in his hide. He's pure mercury on hooves, that horse."

"He doesn't look like a mustang, Pa."

"As I heard it, Demon's pa belonged to a Mexican general. The animal was pure Arabian. Horse ran off and joined a herd of mustangs. The Comanches captured Demon as a colt, but they couldn't break his will. He's a world of trouble, that horse. You can't help but admire him, though."

"He'd be hard to run down," I said, watching as Demon pranced before his mares. "Now those others might be easier."

"Just what I was thinking, Alby," Pa said. "And if we work it right, we might even get Demon to do some of our job for us."

I didn't ask how. It was good to see Pa cooking up a scheme. Whatever he figured was fine by me.

Before we went to making plans, Pa moved about the camp, stirring the others to life. Uncle Mitch took one glance at the horses and scowled.

"That devil horse nearly killed you once, Frank," he complained. "You don't mean to have another try at him, do you?"

"Thought I might," Pa admitted. "Or shoot him for the bounty."

"Oh, you'll do that, will you?" Uncle Mitch asked sarcastically. "No real horseman will ever kill Demon," he said, looking at me in particular. "No, J. T. will be old and gray before Demon stops running across this country."

Nebo threw off his blanket then, and it wasn't long

before he had some breakfast ready. There were strips of bacon and corn cakes enough for twenty people. We six didn't leave so much as a crumb.

By the time the sun was up proper, Demon's herd had moved along to the north. Pa didn't seem worried about that. He mounted his horse and led Uncle Mitch off into the distant hills.

"You boys break down the camp," he instructed before leaving. "Get the wagon ready to move."

We did as ordered. It didn't take long, and we passed what seemed like an eternity waiting on that hillside. Matt and I took turns riding out to have a look, but neither of us spotted Pa or Uncle Mitch. The Flats appeared to have swallowed both of them.

Eventually Uncle Mitch returned to lead us northward.

"We'll be settling for a time," he told us. "Frank's found the perfect place."

I had no notion of what that might be. Matt and J. T. were equally puzzled. As for Nebo, well, he didn't seem to care. His coughing had stopped when the air warmed, and he trusted Pa to do what was needed.

We wove our way through a series of valleys cut by one creek or another. Eventually we came to a small draw enclosed by hills on three sides. A winding creek cut through the center of it.

"A natural corral," Uncle Mitch pointed out. "Good water, too. We just build ourselves a fence across the mouth of it, and we have a perfect place for holding the horses."

"It's awfully big," I said, scratching my head. It was close to a hundred yards deep and nearly as wide in places. You could fit three of Demon's harems inside.

It narrowed at its mouth, but we still had forty yards to close.

"See those cottonwoods yonder?" Uncle Mitch said, pointing to the tall trees lining the stream.

"I see 'em," I answered.

"Get some axes and start felling them. Strip off the bark and set what's left off the ground, so it can dry. Later we'll split them. Make good fence rails."

"You sure you want to use those trees?" I cried. "They're awfully big!"

"It'll take big trees to hold these ponies," Pa insisted as he joined us. "I want a rail fence across the mouth of this draw. A strong one. Leave a gate wide enough to allow a big herd through. Make it so you can close it easily."

"Well, it sounds simple enough," Matt said, shaking his head.

"Ever cut down a tree half as tall as those cottonwoods?" I asked. "Fifty feet!"

"I never chopped anything more'n an inch or so wide," Matt admitted. "We need a saw."

"Or a cannon," Nebo added. "Since we've brought neither, I suggest we go to work."

We did just that. From sunup to sundown we slaved away, building the fence. The big, single-bit axes that Pa had brought were perfect for stripping bark and trimming small limbs. They were less effective cutting across the girth of those cottonwoods.

Matt and I did most of the chopping. Hard as it was, I think I favored it over the rail-splitting. You could judge some progress when a tree crashed to earth. No sooner than the fallen tree gave way to the splitter, we added the rails to the fence.

84

Three days we toiled on that fence. Our only break came each afternoon when we splashed away some of our weariness in the creek. Then we'd return to work.

In spite of the cold, I began welcoming dusk. Nightfall ended our labors and left us a short interval after dinner to swap stories or sing a bit. Matt brought along his ma's fiddle, and he played a tune or two for us. Nebo also took a turn. He wasn't up on the classical songs like Matt, but for a rousing melody, you couldn't top Nebo.

After we slid the last rail into place, Pa announced that we needed a working corral just outside the draw. This time we settled on a small section of grass near the creek. We sank posts in the hard, rocky ground and then tied ropes from post to post. It made an adequate corral.

When Pa satisfied himself that everything was ready, he gathered us together.

"I tracked Demon this morning," Pa said. "I know just where he is. We'll get him to lead his whole herd right into our little draw here."

"How?" I asked.

"I confess it will be a challenge, but here's how we'll do it."

We grinned as he spelled out his plan. We'd have one last peaceful night. Then the real work would begin.

That next morning Pa roused us even earlier than usual. I rolled over and tried to ignore him, but he'd developed a talent for poking and prodding boys with that crutch of his. A whack here and a poke in the ribs, and I reluctantly got to my feet. Nebo had bacon crackling in a frying pan, and the aroma stirred me to

85

life. I shook myself awake, pulled on my overalls, and stumbled to the fire. Matt followed in a few moments, and J. T. dragged himself over a hair later.

"Eat hearty, boys," Nebo urged as he filled our plates.

"Good advice," Uncle Mitch added. "We'll be a time riding today. You'll need every ounce of strength you can muster."

"That's a cheering thought," Matt said between bites of corn cake. "Sore as I am, it's bound to be worse tomorrow."

"Suspect it will be," I told him. "But maybe we'll have the horses."

I hoped so. If not, who could say what kind of misfortune we'd meet? Pa's plan was grand—too grand by half, Uncle Mitch thought. Matt and I had big parts to play, and we grew more nervous by the moment. As we saddled our horses, I found myself envying J. T. and Nebo, who stayed in camp. All they had to do was slide the rails in place after we drove the mustangs into the draw.

"It's not as easy as it sounds," Matt warned when I grumbled about it aloud. "They'll have forty or fifty horses thundering down on them, dust everywhere, and no kind of shelter. If they're not quick enough, those horses will run back and trample them."

I nodded soberly. I couldn't see where they were worse off than we were. Pa and Uncle Mitch would ride ahead of us. It was their job to stampede the herd, to direct them to the draw. Matt and I would close in behind, waving blankets and pressing them onward. If any horse had the gumption, and at least one of them had plenty, we might find ourselves on the opposite side of hundreds of flying hooves.

"There's something else, too," Matt told me. "These ponies of ours might just choose to join their brothers and sisters. They're not all that used to riders, remember?"

That was, as Matt pointed out, no cheering thought.

I didn't dwell on all the things that might go wrong. After all, as Matt told me, "If we're dust, we're dust." In truth, I trusted my pony to go where I told him, and I didn't think Demon could be as clever as Pa said.

"He's likely old if you chased him back in the '50s," I'd said. "If those mares are half the bother the Hester sisters are, Demon might welcome us."

When I got a good look at Demon that morning, every humorous notion left my mind. He was as big and fearful a horse as Pa said, and he showed no sign of age. We were still a quarter mile away when he saw us. Almost immediately he was galloping out, screaming defiantly as he reared himself up on his hind legs.

"I know how he got his name," Matt remarked.

"Name's only part of it," Uncle Mitch said. "Frank, any change of plans?"

"No, we do it just like I said," Pa replied. "Alby, you and Matt ride over to that rise yonder and stay put. If we can turn the herd south, follow. Ride hard and scream to high heaven. Wave those blankets. Don't ease up or the mustangs will slip away in pairs. You understand?"

"We'll do it," I promised.

"Just try your best," Uncle Mitch added. "Be alert. If the whole herd turns, get clear of them."

I nodded, but I didn't see how we could drive the horses and be careful at the same time. The concern etched on my uncle's forehead told me he didn't think we could, either. Pa, on the other hand, appeared calm. He insisted on checking our saddles. He leaned over and assured himself the cinches were tight.

"You've a man's task ahead of you," he told me. "It's not fair to hit you this early, but then you've shouldered a burden since '61."

"I won't let you down, Pa," I assured him.

"Don't worry, son. We'll get it done."

Matt and I rode toward the rise while Pa and Uncle Mitch approached Demon from opposite directions. The big stallion appeared confused for a moment. He finally moved toward Pa, but Uncle Mitch shouted and charged. Demon turned back, only to have Pa charge. With men rushing him from two sides, Demon hesitated. Then he galloped straight ahead, toward the draw and its fence.

Matt and I watched in awe at the way Pa and Uncle Mitch drove Demon southward. They dashed across the front of the herd, taking care to avoid the maelstrom of hooves and horseflesh. We waited for the stragglers to pass. Then I waved my blanket and slapped my pony into a gallop. Matt did the same. With blanket-waving madmen at their tails, the mustangs had few choices. Most would have followed Demon anywhere, but a few broke away here and there. It couldn't be helped.

"Ignore them," Pa had instructed, and we did.

After the first mile, I was past thinking. I was caught up in a whirlwind of choking dust, near blinded, and continuing on by instinct more than plan. I lost track of Matt. I couldn't see Pa or Uncle Mitch. I just kept riding and waving that fool blanket. I didn't know anything else to do.

Before long, we approached familiar ground. I saw the hillside where we'd passed our first night on the Flats. Farther ahead I saw the smoke from Nebo's cook fire. We were soon racing along on either side of the creek, galloping wildly toward the draw.

I felt my heart pounding, and I did my best to steel myself against the quick stop that was coming. I knew as well as anyone what a sudden halt on a freshly broken pony meant. Like as not, my mustang would buck me right over his nose and leave me in the swirling dust.

It didn't happen. I spotted Nebo and J. T. sitting atop the fence on either side of an opening. J. T. waved his hat, and I waved my blanket in return. The horses were charging blindly down the draw, but I nudged my pony toward safety. I raced past the fence like a thunderbolt, but I managed to escape.

Matt did a little better—at least for a moment. He pulled away earlier, so he merely slowed his pony and waited for the rails to close. That was when Demon saw his chance.

No wild horse stayed free so long without reason. Demon eyed his chief tormentors and made the fastest turn I'd ever seen. Uncle Mitch couldn't match it, and Pa didn't, either. Demon charged right at Matt, who froze. Those next few seconds seemed like hours. That devil horse was headed right for my best friend, and I turned my pony without thinking. I then raced across the rocky ground, howling and screaming like a banshee. The noise broke Matt out of his trance, and he dodged away. My sudden arrival blocked Demon's escape, and he reluctantly moved back to his harem. The last few mares were passing the gate, and Demon

89

dashed through to join them. Nebo and J. T. closed the rails, and the herd was ours.

"We did it!" Pa shouted.

"We showed 'em, didn't we?" Uncle Mitch yelled.

I glanced at Matt, who coughed dust out of his mouth.

"I'm glad that's over," he said, letting out a long breath.

It wasn't over, though. Not by half.

Standing outside the fenced draw was a little like walking alongside a lit keg of gunpowder. For close to half a day Demon and his harem tested the strength of our fence. First one horse would throw itself against the rails. Then another tried. Demon himself tried to climb the steep slope of the confining hills. Pa had picked a good spot, though. The mustangs were trapped.

Once the dust had settled, and it took some time, Nebo cooked us up something to eat. We tried to shake off some of the soreness we all felt from our wild ride. I suppose I was stiff as anybody. I sure ached! But for me, the dust and dirt covering every inch of me were the real plague. I walked down to the little creek and jumped in.

"Fellow's supposed to take his clothes off before taking a bath, Alby!" Matt scolded.

"My clothes are as dirty as I am," I argued. "I need to get them clean, too."

That was all the persuading J. T. needed. He ran over and jumped in beside me. Matt followed.

"Ah, fudge and cherries," Nebo said, abandoning his kettle and the pile of dirty plates. A moment later there were four of us in the creek.

"There's work waiting," Pa called.

"It can keep," Uncle Mitch said, laughing. "To be truthful, Frank, I could shed some dust myself."

Before any of us quite knew what was happening, Pa and Uncle Mitch headed for the creek, too. You'd expect Mitch to make good time, but Pa was amazing. He used the crutch for balance, but he mainly hopped along like a frog.

"Told you you'd get the hang of that stick, Frank," Nebo said as Pa dropped himself into the shallow stream.

"You've been right about a lot of things, Nebo," Pa admitted. "And I've been wrong about more than I can remember."

It was as close to an apology as we were apt to get. I managed a grin, and J. T. helped Pa peel off his clothes. When I removed mine, I was shocked to see dust underneath as thick as that on the outer part of me.

"How'd it get through my clothes?" I asked, mystified.

"Give it to Texas," Matt said, amazed to discover his back coated with grime. "It's even dustier here than anywhere else."

That wasn't all. We were peppered with sand flea bites, and mosquitoes had eaten their fill. I pulled two ticks off J. T.'s neck.

"We'd best give our shelter a floor," Nebo suggested. "Make it a little harder for the bugs to eat us."

We all agreed that it was a fine idea, although none of us knew when we'd find the time to do it.

We washed dust and dirt from our weary bodies and then hung out our clothes to dry. Fortunately, the sun was shining, so that for once I didn't feel a chill. We were an odd sight, the six of us walking around naked as newborns. I confess I felt a little shy about that. It was hard on Nebo, too, what with all his scars. Pa hopped off by himself for similar reasons. None of us save Nebo had ever seen his bare stump. He always tied his trousers up so no one had to.

"It's only flesh," Nebo said when J. T. shrank from the sight. "Just appears odd because the bone's gone."

"It's raggedy," J. T. said, scowling. "Couldn't the docs have done a better job?"

"No time," Nebo explained. "Frank was lucky. Yankee surgeons took that leg. They had something to knock him out with. Many's the time I heard our boys screaming as the surgeons took out their saws."

I winced at the notion.

"Don't make so much fuss," Nebo pleaded. "He's already shy about it."

I tried to ignore the stump, but that wasn't possible. So instead I walked over and sat with him.

"Would you look at that," Pa said, shaking his head.

"What?" I asked, shrinking under his sharp gaze.

"Here I thought I was surely the most peculiar thing around, and you come along."

"Yeah," I said, laughing nervously. "I'm mostly all legs nowadays."

"That's not what I meant, Alby. Here, what do you feel?"

He took my fingers and ran them along my chin.

"Whiskers," I said, grinning. "I'm finally growing whiskers."

"It's time," he told me. "You're getting to be a man most other ways."

"I've got to show Matt," I said, hurrying off. The moment I left, I was sorry for it. I glanced back and spied Pa's disappointment. He had something more to say. Later, when I gave him the chance to tell me, he seemed a thousand miles away. And Matt had noticed the chin hairs days before.

"Why didn't you say anything?" I asked.

"Figured you'd know what was growing out of your own chin," he grumbled. "Besides, how was I to know they were new? Most fellows shave 'em off regular."

I intended to leave mine for all the world to see.

"Folks'll have to get pretty close," J. T. told me. "Those hairs are like little yellow threads."

Any excitement I felt about growing whiskers faded into memory by afternoon. Once our clothes dried, we dressed ourselves. Pa then set us to practicing with lariats and checking the fence for weak spots.

"We've got a lot of work left to do, and November's closing fast," he said. "I've got you this far because the leg didn't hold me back. No one-legged man alive ever gentled a mustang, though. You fellows have to do the rest."

"We'll start with the mares," Uncle Mitch announced. "Each of us'll pick one. We'll need to geld the stallions, and that will be a job requiring all of us."

I avoided his eyes. Matt winced.

"It can't be that different than with hogs," J. T. said.

"You don't wait for a hog to get big," I pointed out.

"Those horses can pound you into dust, and I don't know I would even hold it against 'em."

"No," Uncle Mitch said, laughing. "I don't suppose the man was ever born who took on such a task without flinching a bit. Like I said before, we'll work the mares first."

I expected we would wait for sunrise to get started, but Pa had us enter the draw that afternoon. We each had our rawhide lariat, and he told us which pony to rope.

"You need to drop two loops over her head," Pa explained. "A man holds her from each side. Nebo, you slide those rails back so they can bring her out."

"Pa?" I asked in alarm as he climbed the rails and aimed his rifle into the herd.

"Best to ward off a rush," he told us. "If they all charge at once, though, forget your lariat. Get clear."

The horses were as weary as we were, though, and Demon was off trying to climb his way out. We looked over the herd carefully. Pa warned that we'd have an easier time with the younger animals, but we couldn't be certain the cavalry would accept such mounts. In the end Uncle Mitch suggested a spry buckskin. We roped her and dragged her toward the gate. It was all I could manage to hold on, and twice the mare pulled Matt off his feet. That buckskin fought us every inch of the way, and when we finally got her safely inside the work corral, I collapsed.

"Next?" Pa called.

"The paint," Uncle Mitch suggested. "The one with the white tail."

Matt and I exchanged looks of disbelief. We were past arguing, though. Once the buckskin settled down, we retrieved our lariats. I took a deep breath and started toward the draw. Matt followed.

The paint made less of a fight of it—in the beginning, at least. I managed to drop my loop over her head on the first try. Matt took two throws.

"Come on, girl," I whispered as Nebo slid the rails back, allowing us to pass through. Once past the fence, that horse reared up and tried to kick my head off. I hung on for all my life while Uncle Mitch raced over and threw a third loop over the paint's head. With the three of us tugging, and occasionally choking the wind out of her, we managed to haul our second horse into the corral.

"Take that black mare next," J. T. suggested. "The one with the splash of white across her face."

I sighed and stared at my toes.

"Get to it," Uncle Mitch demanded.

Matt and I again retrieved our lariats. We headed for the draw, and Nebo slid the rails open. It nearly proved our undoing. The mustangs were waiting, and they flew at us in a rush. I lifted one end of the rail, and Matt threw himself under it. Nebo tried to get to the other, but before we closed the gate, ten ponies escaped.

"Demon?" Pa called.

"No," I told him. "He's still in back, trying to get up the slope."

"Well, we kept most of them anyway," he said, sighing.

I counted thirty-five in the draw. With the two in the work corral, we had thirty-seven.

"That's plenty to keep us busy," Pa noted. "Well, go have a try at that white-faced vixen."

We took no chance with the third mare. Matt and I got our ropes around her neck, and we guided her firmly toward the rails. Pa fired a warning shot, and the other horses retreated while we led out the dark mare. She hardly fought us at all.

"At least one was gentle," I said, sighing. "Next?"

"Three's enough for now," Pa announced. "If we get these three ready by tax time, we keep the farm."

"If the soldiers buy them," I added.

"Alby, you can always sell horses in Texas," Pa assured me. "It may snow in July some year, and John Tyler may even sprout whiskers. Those are only possibilities. A good horse will always fetch a fair price."

Our mustang education then commenced.

Those horses weren't what you'd call graceful. They lacked a thoroughbred's clean lines or proud gait. For pure fury, though, mustangs had no equal. They stood twelve to thirteen hands high, and most of ours were darkish, like Demon. Except for the one with the white face, those ponies were wary of humans. If they had worn brands, I would have guessed they were ill-treated ranch stock.

"Shouldn't we get started?" J. T. asked after a time.

"Can't put it off forever," Pa admitted. "Alby, grab a blanket. You should go first."

I expected Uncle Mitch to show us how, but Pa did most of the instructing.

"You learn by doing, not watching," Pa insisted.

We started with the paint. Matt and Uncle Mitch threw their ropes over her head, and I approached slowly, cautiously. I then draped the blanket over her head. That quieted the mare considerably.

"Take my rope, Alby," Uncle Mitch said. I held it

while he approached the mare's right foreleg. He lifted it and bound it with a short rope. The poor animal wobbled as it tried to adjust to the loss of a leg.

"Here," Pa said, tossing me a halter. "Fit it tight. Once you've finished, throw me the blanket."

"Pa?"

"We're not training a horse to run blind," he told me. "You can hold on to the halter."

I can? I considered asking. Actually, the paint seemed at ease. I climbed atop her and nudged her into motion. We turned two small circles.

"Good, son," Pa said. "See if you can get her to prance."

I thought we were doing just fine as things were, but I did as ordered. The paint complied. Then, quick as lightning, she decided she'd had enough. I felt the animal tense. She arched her back and jumped skyward. Even on three legs she managed to jostle me. I hung on for all my life, and she shook and jumped, twisted and turned. Whenever I eased up on the reins, she grew downright vicious.

"Press your knees into her," Pa urged. "Don't give her the wind to hurt you."

I tried, but I didn't have the strength. The paint threw me into the air and nearly stomped me proper.

I rolled my way free of the corral. J. T. slapped my back, and Matt howled with approval.

"I think I lost that fight," I told them.

"You'll win the next one," Matt assured me.

Uncle Mitch judged my first effort satisfactory and sent me back into the corral to try again. He then concentrated on the buckskin. Matt approached the white face. Soon the work corral was full of pounding hooves and screaming riders.

"Nooooo!" Matt hollered as the white face threw herself against the ropes. Matt rolled off into the dust, and the horse raced away, snorting and stomping.

"Matt?" I called from the paint's back.

"I'm fine," he answered. "Just a little flat on the left side."

Uncle Mitch used a quirt to punish the buckskin's transgressions, and he offered it to me. I couldn't abide beating the spirit out of a horse, though. Instead, I whispered to the mare and stroked her flanks.

Matt tried something different on the white face. He got back atop her and clamped his teeth onto one ear. The horse protested, but each time she fought him, he'd bite a little more.

"Pa used to do it this way," Matt explained. "It worked fair at Colonel Stone's place."

I wasn't convinced. Riding along with your teeth on your pony's ear appeared more than a little peculiar. Besides, I was doing pretty well with the paint.

"Boy's a natural," Uncle Mitch declared. "We may have to try him out on Demon."

My eyebrows nearly rose right off my face.

"Why don't you try the white face first, Alby," Pa suggested. "Maybe she'll respond."

"Be careful," Matt urged as he jumped down. "She's tricky."

"Likely she'll be glad to be free of your teeth."

"No gladder'n I am to be free of her," Matt added.

I got atop the white face and nudged her to the right. She responded. We next went left. I nudged her into a trot, and we circled the corral three times. I was almost ready to dismount when she suddenly reared up and tossed me halfway to next week. I landed on my side with a thump, and the white face whined arrogantly at me.

"Nothing works every time," Uncle Mitch said as he helped me up.

"Guess not," I confessed. "Maybe next time I'll bite an ear."

Mustanging was hard work. From dawn to dusk we labored at gentling those mares. Only the buckskin and the paint were ready before October ended. Uncle Mitch took both to Jacksboro and sold them.

"I only got forty-five for the buckskin, Frank," he told Pa afterward. "I don't think those Yanks appreciate my efforts."

"And the paint?" I asked.

"A colonel bought her. Paid seventy-five dollars."

"More than enough to pay our taxes," I said, sighing with relief. Only then did I learn that Pa wasn't the only one with taxes due. Matt's ma and Uncle Mitch were also counting on our profits. We had just managed enough with the horse money and what Mr. Hutchison paid Ma for the sheep.

"We'll have more when we sell the other horses," J. T. declared.

"Sure," Pa agreed. With winter on the wind, though, we couldn't spend a week on every animal.

"The younger ones will be easier to train," Uncle Mitch reminded us. "Let's work them first."

To give him his due, Uncle Mitch was right about the ponies. They responded well to a firm hand and a little salt. Matt and I gentled them while Uncle Mitch fought the other, better horses. They remained as stubborn as ever, but we had to ready some of them for market. We all knew that the cavalry required larger, stronger mounts.

"These ones just won't respond to mild treatment," Uncle Mitch warned whenever I had a try.

"How's it done, then?" I asked.

"Sometimes it isn't," Mitch told me. "I've seen a man use a whip and spurs, but he often ruins the animal. No one'll turn an animal like Demon into a saddle horse. He's had too long a run."

"Things change," I said. Didn't I know that better than anyone?

Demon did change—in a way. As pony after pony left the draw, the big stallion stormed about, tearing up the ground with his hooves and flaring his nostrils. I couldn't help but feel a little sorry for him. In order to bring my family back together, we were tearing his apart.

November brought frequent visits from Ma and my little brothers. Best of all, Splinter arrived. It seemed like I hadn't tossed him a stick in a coon's age. I knew he was probably in the way at the Flats, but he did cheer me considerably.

Aunt Lottie brought Maureen and Eben out, too. The evenings grew colder, and none of our guests stayed overnight. Still, Ma always provided a welcome relief from Nebo's cooking, and Maureen generally baked us a pie.

"Frank, it's time you sent those boys home," Ma

argued once the first frost struck. "Especially Nebo. Look how pale he's grown. You told me yourself he was bothered by chills."

"We only have a few animals left to break," Pa objected. "It won't be much longer."

"We have a corral at home," she pointed out. "Bring the ponies back. You'll have all spring to work with them."

"It's not a bad idea, Frank," Uncle Mitch added. "That way we can concentrate on the mares."

Pa reluctantly agreed. Matt, J. T., and I threw ropes over the ten likeliest ponies and followed Ma home. Taking into account four horses sold to a Denton rancher and two more sold in Sherman, only eighteen remained at the Flats. Pa planned to keep five of them to replace the pair he returned to Mr. Hester. Our work, it seemed, was coming to an end.

Of course, my figuring didn't include Demon. We didn't truly expect to break him to the saddle. We concentrated our efforts on the others. Between Uncle Mitch's hard work and my coaxing, we got seven more horses to accept riders. Pa rode to Jacksboro himself to fetch the Yank cavalry colonel to Mustang Flats. We boys were back there when they arrived.

The colonel's name was Frank, too. Frank Monroe. He seemed downright eager to purchase our horses.

"Good animals," he told Pa after climbing atop each one in turn. A quartermaster sergeant looked over teeth and hooves and pronounced each mare fit.

"I can offer you forty-five dollars each," Colonel Monroe said.

"That's not exactly top price," Pa observed. "I think a hundred would be closer to their value."

"Maybe, but forty-five is all I'm prepared to pay," the colonel replied. "I have the cost of shoes, after all. And though they're gentle enough now, we all know a mustang's prone to go wild on you again."

"I don't suppose we'll do better," Pa lamented.

"Not in cash money," the sergeant added.

"Now that black up the draw's a real horse," Monroe declared. "I'd pay two hundred dollars for him myself!"

"He's a trial, that one," Pa said, shaking his head. "Won't allow a man with a rope near. You'd have better luck with one of the other stallions. There's a young paint—"

"No, I'd want the black," the colonel said. "Make it three hundred. We'll take the others now, and if you can break that black before the general's inspection tour in two weeks, bring him to Jacksboro."

The soldiers left, taking the mares. Nebo began packing up his cook pots, and I started to take down the canvas shelter.

"Three hundred dollars is a fortune," Pa said, staring hard at Demon. "Let's not be in a hurry to go. I want a crack at that horse myself!"

"Pa?" I gasped.

"Maybe all Demon's been waiting for is a broken-down old soldier like me."

"Frank, that's crazy," Uncle Mitch argued. "Just plain crazy!"

"Well, I've been called worse things in my life," Pa said, laughing. "Maybe he'll kill me, but three hundred dollars seems a big enough price for the risk."

104

It was a high price, all right, but it wasn't worth a man's life. I rose before he did the next morning, borrowed his rifle, and walked to the fence. I had in mind shooting Demon to put an end to such foolish talk. Uncle Mitch stopped me.

"Pa's worth more'n three hundred dollars," I said as I aimed the rifle.

"If it was the money we were talking about, I'd shoot Demon myself," Uncle Mitch replied. "It isn't. You know, Demon's been ridden before."

"What?"

"Your pa roped him. Bound his foreleg like I showed you. Got atop and stayed there."

"I don't understand."

"Demon didn't fight him. It was the oddest thing. The two of them shared something unspoken, like you do with horses. I don't understand it, Alby, and I sure can't explain it."

"But Demon ran away again."

"No, your pa let him go. I don't know why. We weren't long on horses in those days, either. Maybe Frank will tell you about it. He never told me."

"If he rode Demon before, what's he got to prove now?"

"Nothing to you or me or to that Yank colonel. Just maybe, though, he needs to prove to himself that, lost leg or no, he's still Frank Draper."

"You think so?" I asked.

"I think we have to give him that chance, Alby. Don't you?"

I dropped my eyes and lowered the rifle.

I didn't hold out much hope that Pa could climb atop that devil stallion, and he didn't. Demon raced away the moment Pa climbed over the fence. Uncle Mitch and I saddled the two tallest mares, and Matt readied a third horse for Pa. Mounted, the three of us went after Demon. The big stallion danced through the draw, snorting defiantly. He was here, there, everywhere. Finally we tired him enough so Uncle Mitch could get a rope around his neck. I added mine, and Pa threw a third. Uncle Mitch jumped down while Pa and I held the stallion motionless.

"Tie that foreleg good," I urged.

"Count on me," Uncle Mitch replied as he bound the leg. After placing the halter, he climbed atop his mount. Pa slid across and sat on Demon's sweat-streaked back.

"Well, old friend?" Pa said, stroking the big horse's neck.

We had two ropes around that horse, and he only had three feet free. None of it mattered. Demon raged and stormed. In an instant he tore one rope from my hands and nearly dragged Uncle Mitch from his horse. Pa hung on for life as Demon began bucking. That horse hopped in one direction, then another. I'd never seen such a show. Pa clung stubbornly to the animal's back close to five minutes. Then Demon threw him.

I raced over in order to shield Pa from the devil horse's dangerous hooves.

"I didn't do such a good job at it, eh, son?" Pa asked.

He was bruised and battered, but he assured me that no bones were broken.

"I'll be fine," he assured me. "I'm finished gentling horses, though."

"Nobody's ever going to gentle that devil," I argued.

Uncle Mitch insisted on having a try, though. He tried every trick he knew to work the meanness out of that horse. Then he mounted, and the devil horse tolerated him close to a minute. Then the stallion exploded into a frenzy of odd maneuvers. Mitch tumbled off one side and landed hard on the dusty ground.

"Five hundred's a more fit price for this one!" Uncle Mitch hollered.

"I suppose it's my turn now," I announced.

"No, Alby!" Pa shouted.

"Alby, stop!" Uncle Mitch shouted.

They weren't either one of them in a position to halt me. I eased my horse alongside and jumped atop the devil horse. Actually, Demon hardly flinched. There was a wondrous sense of power sitting atop that magnificent horse, and I nudged Demon into motion.

"Pa rode you once," I whispered. "I won't break your spirit, nor hurt you, either."

Demon clawed at the ground. I felt as though he understood, but he was just playing with me. He reared up on his hind legs and charged the fence.

"Alby, jump!" Pa cried.

"Jump, Alby!" Matt screamed.

I wasn't sure whether Demon planned to vault the fence or what. I hugged the giant horse's neck and prayed for the best. At the last instant, Demon broke to the left, bucked hard, and sent me flying.

Now there are probably a thousand places in Texas a boy wouldn't want to land. There are anthills and dung heaps and sharp rocks eager to slice you open.

But except for a nest of thorny locust trees, I can't imagine anything worse than pencil cactus. That's where I landed, bottom first. I imagine people heard my howl in Philadelphia!

I lay there close to five minutes, calling Demon every vile name I could recall. Matt eventually got to me.

"First you go and sprout whiskers," he told me. "Now you've grown spines."

"Have your laugh," I replied. "You try landing in this stuff sometime. It's far from enjoyable."

"Is funny, though," Matt insisted. "You'd agree with me if you didn't have so many spines in you."

"Well, they won't leave of their own accord," I said, plucking two from my forearm. They were wicked things, those spines. They left a sort of stinging barb behind that plagued a fellow for days.

I passed the better part of that afternoon stretched naked across Nebo's wagon bed while he and Pa plucked spines from my abused backside. What made it worse was knowing it was a story they'd be telling until I was old, gray, and very tired of hearing it.

The following day Uncle Mitch had a final try at Demon. He used his bullwhip to quell the stallion's defiance. Even so, the big black refused to allow a rider. Uncle Mitch and Matt finally freed Demon's foreleg. No one else planned such a foolish undertaking as climbing atop that horse.

We gathered for what all of us expected would be the final time that night around a blazing fire. Matt and Nebo took turns fiddling. I sang along when I felt like it. Mostly I lay on my belly and stared out toward the draw where Demon continued to race the wind.

"It's too bad, isn't it, Pa?" I asked. "Three hundred dollars is a lot of money."

"Seems like a lot," he answered. "But Demon would have made a poor saddle horse. I can't see him letting a Yank colonel atop him if he throws such good Texans as us."

"No self-respecting mustang would," Uncle Mitch agreed. "As for the money, well, there's still the ranchers' bounty."

"What?" J. T. cried.

Pa waved Uncle Mitch silent, but Matt and I already knew about it.

"The stockmen of Denton County got together fifty dollars," Matt explained. "Most of them have lost horses to Demon, and they've offered a reward for killing him."

"Killing?" J. T. asked.

"People have thought that they had him captured half a dozen times," Matt said. "Each time Demon got away and went back to his old habits."

"I guess you planned to shoot him all along," I said, staring hard into Pa's eyes.

"I told you about the bounty, Alby," he reminded me.

"We can't very well let a wild stallion loose to run off our neighbors' horses," Uncle Mitch said.

"I thought you believed in leaving the neighbors to their own business," I shouted. "Besides, those Denton County people probably don't even have fifty dollars."

"They do," Pa insisted. "Ten five-dollar banknotes rolled into a tin are sitting in the sheriff's office."

"Oh," I said, sighing. "Well, I guess shooting would be easier than breaking him."

"Be a little like killing myself, though," Pa told us. "Actually, a lot like it."

I didn't like the sound of that one bit. No, sir. I vowed not to let it come down to Pa and that horse.

12

I didn't sleep much that night. I tossed and turned a lot. Pa fared no better. He cried out in the night more than once, and I knew he was remembering the war again. Fifty dollars was a lot of money, especially during hard times, but I wondered if it was worth having the nightmares come back.

Daybreak found me pondering that. Everyone else remained asleep, so I slipped out from under my blanket, threw on my clothes, borrowed Pa's rifle, and returned to the fence. It was oddly quiet there. Later an eerie wind came wailing over the land, and I grew uneasy.

"Maybe you are the devil," I said, gazing at Demon. Once he had been surrounded by mustangs. The mares were gone now. So were the colts. A handful of stubborn stallions remained, but they were no longer afraid of Demon.

He pranced fretfully. Then he stepped closer. Those eyes, which had held such a fiery gaze, seemed almost sorrowful. They couldn't miss seeing the rifle, but I spied no trace of fear.

"The bounty, huh?" Nebo asked. He climbed the fence and sat on the top rail. "Fifty dollars is a lot of money. Today, it's probably worth more than the fifty they gave me when I signed up with the army. I was just a fool of a boy, though. Fourteen and too stupid to think things through. Besides, I didn't have much choice. Pa was dead already, and Ma was sick. I didn't have a farm to call home like you do."

"Must have been bad," I said, avoiding his somber eyes.

"I shared some of it before," he reminded me. "Not all."

"Huh?"

"I told you how they shot me, how a shell knocked me senseless."

"Yes."

"It wasn't that way, Alby. I was scared to death. At Franklin we sent line after line at the Yanks, and whole rows of us fell like wheat before a scythe. A minié ball clipped my ear. That was enough. I ran like a jackrabbit as far and as fast as I could."

"Till the shell hit you."

"That was later," he explained. "At Nashville. Your pa didn't take me to his regiment. I came on my own. Frank offered to patch my ear, so I stayed."

"But weren't you missed?"

"Alby, there wasn't enough of my company left to count. The whole army was a shambles. We went to Nashville like I said, but we were already walking corpses. When the Yanks attacked, I froze like before. Shells and balls hit all around me, and I ran. That scar on my side? A Tennessee lieutenant did it when he tried to stop me running."

"What?"

"I'm a coward, Alby. I lay in a ditch and let them shoot my friends. I wanted to jump up, help with the fighting, but I couldn't. Then Frank came over and grabbed me by the shoulder."

"Was he mad?"

"Mad?" Nebo asked, calming down. A smile flooded his face, and he took a deep breath. "Sergeants run the army, Alby. Your pa could have been a colonel maybe if he'd wanted, but he stayed with the boys, kept the lines straight and steady. When things went crazy, he picked me right up and carried me off the battlefield."

"Well, he's always been a brave man."

"That's when they shot him," Nebo added. "He was saving my life, and I got him crippled. Know why he went and did it?"

"I guess he felt responsible, being a sergeant and all."

"That wasn't it, Alby. Frank said, 'I've got a boy no older'n you back home. Thank God he's there and not here. I hope he never has to see this hard a day.' I guess maybe you are seeing that sort of day, though."

"It's difficult to know what's the right thing to do, Nebo."

"You're lucky, Alby. You got a pa you can ask."

"Do I?"

"Yes," Pa announced as he joined us.

"I told him, Frank," Nebo said solemnly. "I figured he ought to know."

"Does it change anything?" Pa asked. "I'm still missing a leg."

"You've got a crutch," I told him. "And when the

113

ground's too rough for it to help, maybe you'll let me give you a hand."

"Shouldn't be a son's job, Alby."

"Well, who can say what sort of job I'll have next?"

"Sure," he agreed. Nebo left us alone, and Pa spoke for the first time to me about the war, about the terror that haunted him even then.

"A hundred times I wanted to die," Pa admitted. "Especially after that shell took my leg. One thing kept me going. Your ma and you boys."

"And Nebo," I added.

"My new leg," Pa said, grinning. "He says I pulled him out of a trench, but I don't remember it. I think it was somebody else. We just woke up in the hospital alongside each other. Mitch says it's been hard on you, Nebo coming back with me, but where else could he go?"

"I know, Pa. You couldn't leave him to fend for himself."

"Should have talked with you before about Nebo. About other things, too. When I left, you were just a little boy. Now you've stretched yourself tall, and I'm a stranger. Didn't feel right. And I guess I was too full of my own pain to allow anybody else a mistake."

"I tried to—"

"You didn't do anything wrong, son. You did most of it better than anybody had a right to expect. Hard times come, and they stomp on all of us. We'll pay off our debts and make a fresh start come spring. Who knows? We might run down a few more ponies and start breeding them."

"I wouldn't mind."

"First, though, you've got some deciding to do."

"Yes, sir," I said, staring at Demon. The devil beast seemed smaller somehow, less terrifying. His back bore whip marks, and I spied for the first time the gashes left by the other stallions' teeth.

"I'm not the only one grown old, am I?" Pa asked.

"You're not either of you so old," I argued. "Mrs. Price says a fellow with ears to listen can always learn."

"Well, she's right about that, son."

"Besides, Demon was king of these hills, Pa. Maybe he's ready to settle down after all. We could have another try at him."

"He's too old, Alby. He'll never make a proper saddle horse. An animal like that's got to give his heart to a man. You have to get them young, like those colts."

"You had your chance with Demon."

"Yes, I did, Alby. I think I chose right. What do you think?"

"I don't know, Pa. What about the bounty?"

"You need money that bad? I don't."

"It's not right to keep him here, though," I said. "Look how the other horses treat him."

"It's their turn to rule the range, Alby. It's the same with people. You and J. T. will soon be heading out on your own, planting your own crops and raising your own sons."

"Not for a time yet," I said, leaning against his shoulder.

"Need a hand with the fence rails?"

"Sure."

When we touched the top rail, Demon began prancing around. He snorted and stomped. When we eased that rail out of place, the big black charged. Demon, old and scarred as he was, leaped right over and raced onto the ground beyond. We were so surprised that we barely got the rail back up and prevented the other stallions' escape.

"Well, imagine that!" Nebo called from camp. "Never thought that old horse had it in him."

"We old-timers'll surprise you now and then," Pa declared.

I grinned. As Demon swept across the valley and vanished from view, I couldn't help thinking how some things do change. But not everything.

G. Clifton Wisler is the author of more than sixty books for children and adults. Among his titles are *Red Cap*, an ALA Best Book for Young Adults, and *Mr. Lincoln's Drummer*. He lives in Plano, Texas.